QUANTUM EDGE

THE ENIGMA OF
LADONNA STONE

Written By
ARIES BLACKSTONE

Book Editor & Designer
TESSY OGIDI

DEDICATION

This book is dedicated to my daughter Ladonna, who has been one of the guiding lights of my life and the source of my inspiration for this book. She is brilliant, full of kindness, courage and creativity. She and my family have taught me so much about love, joy, and gratitude. I am proud to be her father and to share this story with her and the world. Ladonna, you are one of my greatest gifts, and being your father is a great honor. Thank you for being you.

"To my beloved wife and our cherished children, your love and patience inspire me daily. You are the anchor in my life and the driving force behind every endeavor. It's for you that I strive harder, dig deeper, and aim higher. I hope to make you as proud of me as I am grateful for each of you."

66

As rivers carve their path to the sea,
Through pain and joy, we come to be.
Forged in the crucible of life's trial,
Is the resilience of the human smile.

99

"The Book of All Collected Knowledge"

WORDS FROM THE AUTHOR

Hello, this is Aries Blackstone, and I'm ecstatic to have you as a reader of my book! Writing is a new adventure for me, even though I've always been a talkative person. Just ask my family! I love creating stories, but it's also nerve-wracking to share them with the world. This book, "Quantum Edge: The Enigma of Ladonna Stone", is my debut novel, but it won't be the last one if I can help it. The saga will continue in the sequel.

I hope you have a blast reading this book. Thank you so much for your time and attention. It means the world to me.

Best wishes!

ONE

Rain battered against the towering glass windows of Skyspire Tower. The sombre rhythm mirrored the tense atmosphere inside the opulent boardroom. Ladonna Stone, a woman veiled in mystery, commanded the attention of all as she sat poised at the head of the table. The board members' eyes betrayed a mixture of curiosity, suspicion, and a touch of envy fixated on this unfamiliar figure about to assume the role of CEO at Quantum Innovations—the tech giant of unparalleled stature. By her side stood T.L. Cline, the outgoing CEO; his weathered countenance, a testament to a life dedicated to the corporate world, bore a hint of admiration and intrigue.

"Ladies and gentlemen of the board," Mr Cline's voice echoed through the room, commanding attention as he stood before the esteemed gathering. The air within the room crackled with anticipation as palpable energy fueled the curiosity of each board member. "Today, I stand before you to introduce a woman who has redefined my perception of brilliance and innovation. Allow me to present to you your new CEO, a true force of nature whose accomplishments will leave you in awe: Ladonna Stone."

A hushed silence filled the room as Mr Cline's words hung in the air. The mystery surrounding this enigmatic figure was shrouded in whispers and speculation. With an unwavering gaze, Mr Cline continued with a voice carrying a mixture of reverence and admiration, "Ladonna Stone, a name that has remained hidden in the shadows, emerges now to claim her rightful place at the helm of this remarkable organization. Her journey has been one of relentless pursuit; a path illuminated by brilliance and unparalleled expertise."

The room remained captivated with each member leaning in to catch every word. Their skepticism transformed into a burning curiosity. Mr Cline's eyes sparkled with intrigue and disbelief. His voice carried a cadence that hinted at the extraordinary tale about to unfold. "Before Quantum Innovations, Ladonna was a hidden gem within the depths of the Department of Defense, handpicked after graduating from the illustrious MIT with a perfect 4.0 GPA—a feat rarely achieved by mortal minds."

There was a collective gasp when they heard her achievement. The sheer audacity of such an accomplishment left the board members astounded. Mr Cline held their attention firmly with his voice brimming in excitement as he peeled back the layers of Ladonna's intellectual prowess. "But it does not stop there. Ladonna Stone holds not one but multiple doctorates across an outstanding array of fields. She holds a doctorate in quantum physics from Harvard University where she studied the emerging field of quantum science and engineering. She also holds degrees in Neuroscience, Biochemistry, Biophysics, Bioengineering, Astronautical Engineering, and yes, she even dabbled into Architecture as if to demonstrate her ability to reshape the very foundations of possibility."

The room became energetic as the feat attained by Ladonna's intellectual prowess rippled through the minds of those present. Ladonna had pursued multiple Doctorates degrees simultaneously, pushing the boundaries of human capability. However, what Mr Cline did not say was that Ladonna's Intelligent Quotient (IQ) was measured between 290 and 350. This set her apart from the mere mortals who surrounded her, while her photographic memory granted her a command over information that defied reason.

Mr Cline continued, "It is not solely her academic achievements that make Ladonna Stone a force to be reckoned with," he added. "Her name and likeness have been cast into the shadows due to the nature of the highly classified projects she developed and worked on within this sector. It is precisely these exceptional qualities and abilities that make her the perfect candidate to guide Quantum Innovations into a future teeming with innovation and triumph."

The whispers swirled like a storm as questions and doubts entwined in a dance of intrigue. Who was this woman, and what secrets propelled her to this precipice of power? Ladonna, unyielding under the weight of scrutiny, met their gazes with an unwavering confidence, the enigmatic depths of her light brown eyes sparked curiosity. Ladonna was as beautiful as she was intelligent. Her heritage, a fusion of Black and Asian lineage, bestowed upon her an allure that transcended superficial boundaries. Yet, it was clear that her mixed-race background alone could not account for the enigmatic circumstances that had elevated her to this position. Ladonna carried within her an intangible enigma, a puzzle that ignited the board members' desire for answers.

As the whispers gradually surrendered to silence, Ladonna rose from her seat, with her voice like a symphony of unwavering authority, she said, "I extend my gratitude to you, Mr Cline, for your kind introduction." Her words were calculated and deliberate. "Accepting the role of CEO at Quantum Innovations is an honour that humbles me. I pledge to lead this company with transparency, integrity, and an unrelenting pursuit for excellence."

The room breathed tension, palpable enough, as board members leaned forward, eager to unravel the enigma that now controlled their fates. Ladonna's lips curved into a subtle smile, a harbinger of revelations about to be unleashed.

"I stand before you as a testament to ambition, resilience, and unyielding determination," Ladonna declared. Her voice commanded the undivided attention of all present. "My journey has been forged in the fire of challenge, propelling me to test the boundaries of what is deemed possible." Her gaze swept the room like a laser beam, capturing the soul of each board member.. "From my earliest days, I obtained the power that knowledge and the embrace of diversity hold. Growing up in a multi-cultural family, I learned of traverse different worlds, adapting, and excelling in each. This mosaic of experiences and perspectives, this kaleidoscope of diversity, is the unique offering I bring to the table as the new CEO of Quantum Innovations."

Furthermore, with words weaved in a tapestry of purpose and promise, she stated, "The allure of technology has always beckoned to me for it possesses the extraordinary ability to mold and reshape the world we inhabit. And within the realm of Quantum Innovations,

I perceive an unprecedented opportunity to propel us further beyond the frontiers of possibility. I assure you, my appointment as CEO was no arbitrary decision. It is a testament to the burning passion that fuels my very being, to my proven track record of accomplishments, and to my unrelenting commitment to excellence. I stand here, ready to lead Quantum Innovations into a future that will surpass the boundaries of imagination."

As she concluded her speech, she stepped back and said, "I invite each and every one of you to join me on this journey. Together, we will redefine what it means to be at the forefront of innovation. Together, we will shape the future."

With these words, she sealed her fate, embarking on a journey that would push the limits of technology, unravel the mysteries of the enigmatic woman at the helm, and propel Quantum Innovations toward an unprecedented destiny. The room erupted in a surge of applause; the echoes of a new era walked through the jubilant boardroom —

a crescendo of anticipation for the thrilling chapters yet to unfold.

However, among the applauding members, was Robert Westfield, whose eyes showed aggression and condescension. This revelation by Ladonna was an affront to his ambitions, a usurpation that would not go unanswered. As the applause settled, Robert's mind raced, calculating his next move. He knew he couldn't afford to underestimate the woman who now held the reins at Quantum Innovations. This was a battle for dominance, and Robert was determined to emerge victorious, no matter the cost.

Robert's aggression and condescension were not mere quirks of his personality; they were the result of a lifetime of struggle and ambition. Born into a family of modest means, Robert had clawed his way up the corporate ladder with a relentless determination that often bordered on ruthlessness. His rise through the ranks had been meteoric, but it had come at a cost. His appointment as Vice President of Business Development had been the crowning achievement of his career, and he had set his sights on the CEO position. The introduction of Ladonna Stone, a virtual unknown, as the new CEO was a slap in the face, a betrayal that cut deep.

Raising his hand, Robert, Quantum Innovations' Vice President of Business Development, interrupted the applause on a voice of derision. "If I may, Mr Cline," he said, "I find it quite intriguing that Ladonna Stone, with her illustrious background and extensive qualifications, has remained shrouded in mystery until now." Mr Cline's gaze shifted to Robert, acknowledging his interruption. "What do you mean, Robert?" he asked.

Robert smirked his eyes darting briefly toward Ladonna before returning to Mr Cline. "I mean, we all know how important transparency and trust are in a company of this magnitude. Yet, Ladonna has managed to keep her past achievements and affiliations hidden. I find it quite intriguing that Ladonna Stone, with her illustrious background and extensive qualifications, has remained shrouded in secrecy until now. Surely, someone of her supposed calibre would have left a more substantial imprint on the corporate landscape. It begs the question, of what else she is hiding from us?"

Mr Cline leaned back in his chair as his gaze shifted between Ladonna and Robert. The room fell into an uneasy silence. The weight of Robert's insinuations brought doubts. The other board members exchanged curious glances at what they heard Robert say.

Ladonna's gaze met Robert's, with her expression unyielding. She knew the mendacious game that he was playing, the subtle jabs that were meant to undermine her authority. With a calm yet commanding demeanor, she responded, "Mr Westfield, I understand your reservations and the need for transparency. Rest assured my past achievements and affiliations were not concealed out of deceit or ulterior motives. They were merely a strategic decision ensuring that my focus remains on the future of Quantum Innovations and the challenges that lie ahead."

A murmur of agreement was felt in the room, a testament to the trust Ladonna had already garnered among the board members bar Robert who was not so easily swayed. "Strategic decision or not, Ladonna, we must be fully aware of who we entrust with the leadership of this company. What if there are hidden agenda, undisclosed allegiances that could compromise our future?" Ladonna's eyes narrowed, with a composure unbroken, she replied, "I assure you, Mr Westfield, my loyalty lies solely with the success and integrity of Quantum Innovations. As for your concerns, I invite you and anyone else with doubts to conduct a thorough investigation into my background. Transparency is indeed crucial, and I have nothing to hide."

The challenge became visible, the gauntlet was thrown between Ladonna and Robert. The board members leaned forward, captivated by the brewing power struggle unfolding before them. They knew that the fate of Quantum Innovations was hinged on their decision.

Mr Cline, the seasoned leader who had handpicked Ladonna for this role, interjected with a firm voice, "Robert, I appreciate your concerns, but I have known Ladonna for years, and the board is well aware of her achievements. She has our complete trust. She has already proven her worth to this company. Let us focus on the future and the opportunities that lie before us."

A moment of tension passed as the board members absorbed Mr Cline's words. Robert, whose face spelled frustration, reluctantly acquiesced. It was a temporary setback, but he knew that his ambitions would not be easily extinguished. "As you wish, Mr Cline. But mark my words, the truth will always come to light."

With that, Robert Westfield took his seat. His eyes locked with Ladonna's. With those words, Ladonna solidified her stance, setting the stage for a battle of wits and power that would shape the future of Quantum Innovations. The clash between Ladonna and Robert loomed; their paths would soon intertwine in a web of mystery and ambition.

TWO

The day after Ladonna was appointed CEO, she requested a private meeting with Mr Cline, the outgoing CEO, who had introduced her to the board. She wanted to discuss her observations about Robert's apparent opposition to her appointment and seek Mr Cline's insights into the dynamics at play within the company. She said, "Thank you for taking the time to meet with me, Mr

Cline. I wanted to discuss something that has been on my mind since yesterday's meeting." Mr Cline replied, "Of course, Ladonna, I am here to support you in any way I can. What is troubling you?"

"It seems that Robert, one of the senior executives, has reservations about my appointment. I noticed his skepticism and his attempts to undermine my vision during the meeting. I would like to understand his motivations and gauge the level of opposition I might face," Ladonna opined.

Mr. Cline sighed, leaning back in his chair, his face etched with concern. "Robert is a complex individual. He's been with the company for many years, working his way up from a junior position. His ambition is no secret, and he expected to replace me. Your appointment has undoubtedly bruised his ego."

Ladonna's mind flashed back to Robert's aggressive stance during the meeting, his eyes filled with cold determination. "But why is he so abrasive? What drives him?"

Mr. Cline's eyes narrowed, and he paused, choosing his words carefully. "Robert's past is filled with challenges. He grew up in a tough environment, always having to fight for recognition. His aggressive nature is a defense mechanism, a way to assert control. He's built alliances within the company, particularly with some of the middle managers who share his views. They see your appointment as a threat to their influence."

Ladonna probed further, "Can you tell me more about his upbringing? What shaped him into the person he is today?"

Mr. Cline looked thoughtful. "Robert was raised in a family where success was the only option. His parents were demanding, and he learned early on that he had to fight for everything. That upbringing instilled in him a relentless drive but also a certain ruthlessness.

He's not afraid to step on others to get what he wants."

Ladonna absorbed this information, her mind racing. "Who else might be swayed by Robert? Are there others within the executive team who share his views?"

Mr. Cline's voice dropped to a whisper, and he leaned closer. "Be cautious, Ladonna. There have been betrayals in the past, and the corporate world can be a treacherous place. Robert has been known to align himself with those who can further his ambitions. He's cultivated relationships with some of the board members and has connections with a rival company. His alliances are not always transparent, and his motivations are driven by profit and power."

Ladonna's eyes narrowed, her intellect dissecting the information. "I see. This is a delicate situation. Robert's influence runs deeper than I initially thought. We must be careful in how we approach this. His alliances with a rival company could be detrimental to our projects, especially the Quantum Computer Project."

Mr. Cline nodded gravely. "Indeed, Ladonna. Robert's connections with our competitors could pose a significant risk. His aggressive and condescending manner masks a shrewd mind. He's relaxed in his approach, but don't be fooled. He's playing a long game, and his alliances are strategic."

Ladonna's mind was already formulating a plan. "We must monitor Robert closely and gather evidence of his dealings with the rival company. If he's sharing secrets for profit, we need to uncover it subtly. We cannot afford to tip our hand."

"You're right, Ladonna. We must proceed with caution. Your intellect and ability to circumvent problems will be crucial in this endeavor. I trust you to handle this with the utmost discretion," Mr. Cline affirmed, his eyes reflecting his confidence in her.

Ladonna's face was resolute. "Thank you, Mr. Cline. I will not let you down. We will protect Quantum Innovations and ensure that our projects succeed."

Mr. Cline's expression softened. "I know you will, Ladonna. Robert's resistance to change and his unhappiness with your appointment are obstacles, but I believe in your ability to navigate them. Keep a close eye on him and the others within the executive team. Trust your instincts."

She nodded, absorbing Mr. Cline's words. "I will, Mr. Cline. I have been studying their profiles, and a few names have caught my attention. I would like to discuss their loyalties and their potential impact on the company."

"Certainly," Mr. Cline retorted, ready to delve into the intricate dynamics of the executive team. "Who specifically are you referring to?" The conversation progressed.

Ladonna: "First, Lucy Wei, the Director of Research and Development. I have read remarkable things about her, and I believe she could be a key ally for me. What are your thoughts on her?" Mr. Cline smiled with a glimmer of admiration beaming in his eyes.

"Lucy is a remarkable individual. She has an exceptional intellect and shares your visionary thinking. With a Ph.D. in Quantum Physics, she's been the driving force behind many of our breakthroughs. She is fiercely loyal and deeply believes in the future of Quantum Innovations. Her innovative spirit and dedication to excellence will align perfectly with your vision. I believe you two will make an unstoppable team."

She felt a sense of reassurance. Having Lucy by her side would supply the support she needed to navigate the intricate world of research and development, pushing the boundaries of innovation.

"That is wonderful to hear. I am glad to have Lucy's expertise and loyalty on our side. Now, what about Vivian Ho, our Chief Financial Officer? I need someone I can trust implicitly in managing the financial landscape of the company." Mr. Cline's expression turned serious as he considered Vivian's role within the organization.

"Vivian is another exceptional individual. You have a great eye for people. With an MBA from Harvard and over 20 years of experience in the financial sector, her financial acumen is unparalleled. She's known for her strategic foresight and ability to navigate complex financial landscapes. She fully supports Quantum Innovations' vision and will recognize your genius. You can trust her to safeguard the company's resources and outmaneuver any attempt by Robert to manipulate our finances."

Ladonna's confidence grew as she heard Mr. Cline's assessment. Vivian's partnership would supply the financial stability and insight needed to execute her ambitious plans.

"That is reassuring to hear. I would also like to discuss Jackson Reed, our Chief of Security. I understand the importance of keeping the company's secrets safe. Can I trust him to protect our interests?"

Mr. Cline's demeanor shifted. His tone conveyed the gravity of the matter at hand.

"Jackson is a former Delta Force. His military background has instilled in him a powerful sense of honor, loyalty, and an unwavering commitment to protecting those he serves. He's been instrumental in implementing cutting-edge security protocols and has a keen eye for potential threats. He understands the importance of keeping the company's secrets confidential. He has kept our data and people safe for many years. You can rely on him to ensure the security and integrity of Quantum Innovations."

Ladonna felt a surge of gratitude for Jackson's presence within the organization. With his military training and keen instincts, she knew she could focus on leading the company without the constant worry of external threats.

"Thank you, Mr. Cline. Your insights have been invaluable. With Lucy, Vivian, and Jackson by my side, I believe we can overcome any challenge that lies ahead. Together, we'll shape the future of Quantum Innovations."

Mr. Cline nodded, a sense of pride evident in his gaze.

"Ladonna, I have every confidence in your abilities and the team you've assembled. You have the vision and intelligence to lead this company to unprecedented heights. Trust in your instincts and lean on your allies. Quantum Innovations is in capable hands."

Before Ladonna left the meeting with Mr. Cline, she felt she had to bring up one more thought for his consideration. It was about Justin Allen.

"Mr. Cline, I value your insight. Finally, I would like to discuss one more person. I want to know your opinion on Justin Allen, the manager of the Quantum Computer Research Lab. He holds a Ph.D. in Quantum Mechanics and has been leading the lab for five years. I believe he holds great potential, but I would like to know your thoughts on his reliability and commitment to the project." Also, she continued, "I have noticed the interactions between Robert and the Quantum Computer Project and want to gain your perspective on the matter."

"Justin was instrumental in the project, Ladonna. He's a visionary in his field, having published numerous papers on quantum algorithms. His loyalty to Quantum Innovations is unquestionable, and he's been a driving force behind our advancements. However, Robert, in particular, has been trying to undermine the project and has voiced his skepticism about its worth. Justin's relationship with Robert is strained, and they've clashed on several occasions."

"That was what I suspected. I have reviewed the records and noticed Robert's repeated attempts to halt the project. We must have a team we can trust implicitly. I believe bringing Justin into my confidence about Superposition could help solidify his commitment and ensure his allegiance is unwavering."

"Ladonna, I understand your intentions, but we must exercise caution. The project's success and the security of your research are of utmost importance. We cannot afford any leaks or compromises. Justin's expertise is invaluable, but we must be certain of his discretion."

"I agree, Mr. Cline. That is why I approached you. I trust your judgment, and I believe that by informing Justin discreetly, we can strengthen our team's resolve and protect the project's integrity."

"Ladonna, I see the potential in your breakthroughs, and I know the importance of having a loyal team. Proceed cautiously, and if you believe Justin can be trusted, then I support your decision."

"Thank you, Mr. Cline. I will exercise the utmost discretion in approaching Justin. Together, we will ensure the success of the Quantum Computer Project while safeguarding its secrets."

With their discussion reaching a pivotal point, Ladonna seized the opportunity to address her ongoing work in her private lab.

"There's one more matter, Mr. Cline. As you know, I continue to work on the Superposition problem from the lab at home. With each passing day, I make progress in stabilizing the qubits and eliminating the need for extreme cooling."

Mr. Cline's eyes widened in awe and anticipation.

"Ladonna, your dedication and brilliance are outstanding. The breakthroughs you've achieved have the potential to revolutionize the field of Quantum computing. But we must remain vigilant in protecting your research."

"Absolutely, Mr. Cline. That is why I am considering bringing Justin in as a confidante. I believe his expertise and loyalty can be invaluable in this endeavor. His understanding of quantum algorithms and his innovative approach to problem-solving align perfectly with our goals."

"If you believe Justin is worthy of your trust and capable of upholding the confidentiality of your research, then I support your decision. But remember, Ladonna, we are treading on dangerous ground. The stakes are very high, and our success depends on maintaining the utmost secrecy."

"I understand, Mr. Cline. I will proceed with caution and ensure that our secrets remain hidden from prying eyes. Together, we will usher in a new era of Quantum Computing."

As the meeting ended, Ladonna and Mr. Cline knew that the path ahead was treacherous. They would have to navigate the intricate web of trust and secrecy while battling the opposing forces that sought to undermine their work. The secrets of Superposition were in their grasp; she had a renewed sense of determination. With the support and trust of her allies, she was ready to face any obstacles that came her way. The web of trust she had carefully woven around her would be instrumental in overcoming the challenges and betrayals that awaited her on her journey as CEO of Quantum Innovations.

THREE

The hum of the car engine was a soothing background to Ladonna's thoughts as she drove to work. Her mind was filled with the warmth of the previous night, the smiles of her three children, ages 16, 13, and 11, and the understanding eyes of her husband, Michael.

Arriving home late, she had been greeted with love and understanding. Dinner had been over, but the children's laughter still echoed in the house, and Michael's embrace had been a balm to her tired soul. They all understood her responsibilities, her late nights, and the weight she carried as the new CEO of Quantum Innovations.

Later, after the children were in bed, she had shared her concerns about Robert Westfield, the Senior Vice President of Business Development, with Michael. He had listened, his silence a testament to his faith in her abilities. He knew she would work it out, as she always had. He knew he was married to one of the most impressive people on the planet.

With a sigh, Ladonna pulled into the parking lot, her thoughts shifting to the day ahead. Her appointment as CEO had sent shockwaves through the company, stirring both excitement and apprehension among the employees. To most, she was a mystery, a genius who had come out of nowhere, offered the position by Mr. Cline himself. Rumors circulated about her being behind most of the great advancements in technology over the past 10 years, but no one could say what advancements. She was relatively unknown, yet her reputation as being fair, thoughtful, and direct preceded her.

There was an air of anticipation as Ladonna stepped into her new role and exerted her vision for the company's future. As Ladonna settled into her new position, she knew that building alliances and solidifying her support network would be vital to navigating the challenges ahead. She called for a meeting with Lucy Wei, the Director of Research and Development, to discuss their shared vision and how they could collaborate to propel Quantum Innovations to new heights. The conversation ensued.

"Lucy, I appreciate you taking the time to meet with me. I have been impressed by your achievements and the groundbreaking research your team has conducted. I believe our collaboration will be crucial in driving the company forward." Lucy's eyes sparkled with excitement as she shook Ladonna's hand.

"Thank you, Ladonna, I've heard so much about you. Your reputation as a genius is intriguing, and I'm thrilled to have you as our CEO," Lucy said, her voice filled with genuine enthusiasm. I share your enthusiasm for pushing the boundaries of innovation. I believe that together, we can achieve remarkable things."

Ladonna smiled, feeling an immediate connection. Their conversation flowed effortlessly. Lucy's admiration for Ladonna was evident, and the feeling was mutual.

"That is precisely why I wanted to meet you. I see immense potential in the projects your team is working on, especially in the field of Quantum Computing. I believe we can leverage this technology to revolutionize not only our products but also the entire industry."

"I have often thought about the practical applications of Quantum Computing beyond the theoretical realm. With your expertise and fresh perspective, we could unlock new possibilities and make Quantum Computing accessible to a wider audience."

"Exactly, Lucy. I envision a future where Quantum Computing becomes an integral part of our everyday lives. Let us explore avenues to make our research more accessible and impactful."

Their discussion continued for the remainder of the meeting. Ideas flowed freely as they explored ways to synergize their expertise and amplify the impact of their work. The seeds of a powerful alliance were sown, promising to drive Quantum Innovations to the forefront of technological innovation.

Meanwhile, Ladonna recognized the importance of a strong financial foundation to support the ambitious endeavors of Quantum Innovations. She scheduled a meeting with Vivian Ho, the Chief Financial Officer, to discuss their shared goals and how they could ensure the company's financial stability and growth.

"Vivian, I have been reviewing the financial landscape of the company, and I must say, your expertise in managing resources is commendable. I believe our partnership will be instrumental in securing the necessary funding and allocating resources effectively."

"Thank you, Ladonna. I share your commitment to ensuring the financial wellbeing of Quantum Innovations. With your vision and strategic guidance, we can maximize our resources and secure the funding needed to propel our projects forward."

"Excellent! Let's work together to develop a comprehensive financial strategy that aligns with our long-term goals. We will need to balance innovation and growth with fiscal responsibility to ensure sustainable success." Said Ladonna.

Their meeting delved into the intricacies of budgeting, forecasting, and investment opportunities. Vivian's financial acumen and Ladonna's strategic insights formed a formidable alliance, laying the groundwork for

Quantum Innovations' financial stability and future growth. Vivian's professionalism and financial acumen impressed Ladonna. Vivian's respect for Ladonna's vision was clear, and Ladonna felt a growing sense of partnership.

As Ladonna continued to forge alliances, she recognized the critical importance of safeguarding the company's secrets and intellectual property. The day continued with a meeting with Jackson Reed, the Chief of Security. Jackson's dedication to safeguarding the company's secrets resonated with Ladonna. Jackson's trust in Ladonna's leadership was palpable, and she felt reassured by his commitment.

"Jackson, I understand the immense responsibility that falls on your shoulders. The security of our projects and data is paramount. I want to ensure that we have a robust security framework in place to protect our innovations from any potential threats."

"Thank you, Ladonna. I take this responsibility very seriously. I have dedicated my career to safeguarding valuable assets, and I am committed to upholding the integrity and confidentiality of Quantum Innovations."

"I have complete faith in your abilities, Jackson. We need to stay one step ahead of those who may seek to compromise our research."

Their meeting delved into the specifics of Quantum Innovations' security measures, from data encryption to physical access controls. Ladonna's insistence on thoroughness and Jackson's meticulous attention to detail formed the foundation of a security alliance that would fortify the company against external and internal threats.

As Ladonna's alliances grew stronger, she knew that there were challenges on the horizon. The skepticism and opposition from Robert Westfield, continued to pose a threat to her leadership and the future of Quantum Innovations. She scheduled a private meeting with Justin Allen, the Manager of the Quantum Computer Research Lab, to discuss her concerns and seek his insights into Robert's motivations.

Meanwhile, even as Ladonna was about to start her meeting with Justin, Robert simmered in his office, fuming as he processed the latest updates from his network of spies within Quantum. Ladonna's influence was growing stronger by the day as she rallied more supporters to her cause.

Unable to contain his frustration any longer, he grabbed his cell phone and dialed his old college buddy Daniel, now an executive at rival tech company Marshall Industries.

"She's gaining too much momentum here," Robert vented as soon as Daniel answered. "Ladonna has most of the board eating out of her hand. Her absurd visions of global domination seem to have them all mesmerized."

Daniel chuckled. "Relax, Bobby. We knew it wouldn't be easy wresting control away from her. But we've dealt with upstarts before. Just stick to the plan."

Robert clenched his fist. "I can't just stand by while she steers this company off a cliff! There must be more we can do to undermine her, and quickly."

"Patience, my friend," Daniel purred. "Opportunities will arise to tarnish her glowing image. For now, keep chipping away at her allies. The seeds of doubt we're planting will bear fruit soon enough."

Robert took a deep breath, regaining his composure. "You're right. I'll keep pressing from the inside. But we need to accelerate our timeline. I want that corner office before year's end."

"We'll get there," Daniel reassured. "Ladonna's days are numbered..."

"Justin, I appreciate your dedication to the Quantum Computer Project. Your expertise and commitment have been instrumental in our progress. However, I have reason to believe that some amongst us may be actively working against our efforts. Have you noticed anything that you could shed light on?" Inquired Ladonna.

"Ladonna, I have had my suspicions about one of the executives for some time now. He has made numerous attempts to undermine the project, voicing doubts and raising unnecessary obstacles. It is clear that this person has an agenda that may not align with the success of Quantum Innovations." Said Justin.

"Thank you for sharing your observations, Justin. We must remain vigilant and united against attempts to derail our progress. I believe that we can gain the support of others in the company and overcome any challenge we feel are being posed to hinder our mission."

As Ladonna concluded her meeting with Justin, she felt a renewed sense of purpose. As the day drew to a close, Ladonna reflected on her meetings, the alliances she had forged, and the trust she had earned. She thought back to the night before, to her family's love and understanding, and felt a surge of gratitude.

The battle for Quantum Innovations' destiny was just beginning, but with her trusted allies by her side and the unwavering support of her family, Ladonna was prepared to face whatever challenges lay ahead. The web of trust she was carefully weaving around her would be instrumental in overcoming the challenges and betrayals that awaited her on her journey as CEO of Quantum Innovations.

FOUR

Months had passed since Ladonna's appointment as CEO of Quantum Innovations, and the company had seen significant progress under her leadership. Breakthroughs were made, alliances were strengthened, and her vision was taking shape. Yet, the shadow of Robert's constant attempts to undermine her loomed large. His aggression had grown, fueled by his correct perception of Ladonna's increasing influence within the company and the board.

Robert, known for his aggression and ambition, had become a thorn in Ladonna's side. He had taken every opportunity to undermine her leadership, feeling threatened as she made inroads with the board and other employees. His skepticism had grown into a relentless pursuit to challenge her at every turn.

Just as it was months before, rain poured outside, and the intensity grew fiercely within the boardroom. Ladonna stood at the head of the table with all poise and determination. And there was Robert, a Senior executive with a reputation for aggression. He leaned back in his chair. His smug expression served as a shield for his skepticism. Ladonna had expected this and was ready for the challenges he would raise.

"Good morning, everyone. Today, I want to unveil a vision that will transform Quantum Innovations into an even larger global powerhouse." Said Ladonna.

Robert scoffed under his breath, a derisive smirk playing on his lips. He was ready to undermine Ladonna's authority at every turn.

"I welcome anyone questions and concerns. It is only through open dialogue that we can forge a path to success."

Robert whispered to a colleague, "Do we believe she is the right person for this job?"

His whispered comment to a colleague was a thinly veiled attempt to undermine Ladonna's authority. But Ladonna maintained her composure and locked eyes with him.

"Robert, I sense some skepticism in the room. It is only natural to have questions. Please feel free to voice your concerns."

"Oh, Ladonna, I am glad you are open to questions. After all, we have high expectations for the leader of this company. Forgive me if I am skeptical. We have seen lofty plans before, only to watch them crumble under the weight of unrealistic ambition. What makes you so different?" Said Robert.

"Robert, I understand your reservations. Let me assure you, my vision is not built on empty promises. It is grounded in meticulous research, market analysis, and a profound understanding of our industry's potential. We have the opportunity to revolutionize the tech world."

"Revolutionize? That is quite a lofty word, Ladonna. What challenges do you foresee, and how do you plan to overcome them?"

"Robert, I am glad you asked. Anticipating challenges is a crucial part of our strategy and a major part as to why I was selected as CEO of Quantum Industries. We have conducted thorough risk assessments and developed contingency plans to address any hurdles that may arise. We won't be deterred by obstacles; we will use them as steppingstones to success."

"It is easy to talk about plans, Ladonna. The real test is in execution. Can you deliver on your grand promises?" Or will you crash and burn as others have and take Quantum Industries down with you? Your plan sounds ambitious, but I wonder if it is too ambitious. Have you considered the risks and potential roadblocks?"

"Robert, I understand your skepticism and I respect it. But, I have assembled a team of brilliant minds who share my passion and dedication. We are committed to turning our vision into a reality. The success of this project hinges on our unwavering commitment to excellence. But let me ask you a question, Robert, are you as committed to the success of Quantum Industries as the brilliant minds that are working on this project? We all need to be of one mind here to see to the success of Quantum Industries. Do you agree?"

Robert's dismissive smile faltered for a moment. A glimmer of doubt crept into his eyes. Ladonna's words struck a nerve, challenging his pre-conceived notions. Robert did not respond. His goal was to get Ladonna removed from her position and be appointed as the new CEO.

"Robert, In the face of adversity, we will rise. Together, and only together, will we achieve remarkable things and secure Quantum Innovations' place at the forefront of technological innovation. Trust me, Robert, this is just the beginning." Said Ladonna.

Their tense encounter ended, leaving a lingering tension in the room. Ladonna's measured responses had chipped away Robert's confidence, planting seeds of doubt in his mind. She had defied his expectations, displayed her strategic brilliance, and commanded the respect of those around her.

As the rain continued to pound against the windows, Ladonna stood tall, ready to face the challenges ahead. Shadows of betrayal loomed, but Ladonna's intelligence, foresight, and unwavering determination would guide her through the treacherous path she had chosen. The battle for Quantum Innovations had only just begun, and Ladonna was prepared to face it head-on. The stakes were high, the opposition fierce, but Ladonna's resolve was unbreakable. Her vision was clear, her team was strong, and she was ready to lead Quantum Innovations into a new era of technological innovation.

Meanwhile, unbeknownst to Ladonna and the rest of the Quantum Innovations team, Robert was not idly standing by. His ambition and resentment fueled his secret efforts to undermine Ladonna's authority and further his own interests.

In the confines of his office, Robert paced back and forth, his frustration palpable. His cell phone lay on the desk, its screen illuminated with an incoming call. With a tense exhale, he picked up the call, knowing that the voice on the other end understood his predicament all too well.

"Daniel, this needs to escalate faster," Robert growled into the phone. "Ladonna's gaining too much momentum, and her alliances are making it difficult to maneuver."

Daniel's voice came through, cool and calculating. "Patience, Robert. Rushing this could expose us. We've planted seeds of doubt, and now we wait for them to take root."

Robert's fingers drummed impatiently on the desk. "I don't have time for subtlety, Daniel. The longer she's in power, the harder it'll be to remove her."

Daniel's chuckle was mirthless. "I understand your urgency, but we need to ensure we don't attract attention. Keep undermining her from within, and we'll strike when the time is right."

Robert clenched his jaw, torn between his desire for swift action and Daniel's caution. "Fine, I'll play the waiting game for now. But be ready to move when I give the word."

Daniel's response was a simple, "Of course."

With the call ended, Robert leaned back in his chair, frustration etched into every line of his face. He glanced at a framed photo on his desk – a picture of him, Daniel, and a group of college friends, taken years ago. The memory of their shared ambitions and camaraderie contrasted sharply with the betrayal that now unfolded.

As the days went on, Robert's efforts to sow discord and distrust within Quantum Innovations intensified. He strategically shared misinformation, created doubt about Ladonna's decisions, and manipulated circumstances to his advantage. His interactions with his co-workers became a web of deception, with each move designed to further his hidden agenda.

However, Robert's actions did not go unnoticed. Jackson Reed, the Chief of Security, had a knack for recognizing subtle shifts in behavior and atmosphere. He had noticed Robert's increased interactions with certain employees and the whispers that seemed to follow his presence.

In a quiet corner of the office, Jackson spoke with Ladonna, concern etched in his features. "Ladonna, I've been observing some unusual activities within the company. Robert's been acting more covertly, and there's a sense of tension in certain departments. It's as if he's trying to manipulate the situation somehow."

Ladonna's brow furrowed, her instincts on high alert. "Are you certain, Jackson? If Robert is plotting something, we need to know the details."

Jackson nodded. "I've begun discreetly investigating, but I wanted to make you aware. We can't afford to underestimate him."

As Ladonna absorbed this information, a sense of urgency surged within her. Robert's actions were not just personal attacks; they posed a significant threat to the stability and progress of Quantum Innovations. She knew she had to stay steps ahead, but the complexity of the situation was a stark reminder that her challenges were far from over.

The shadows of betrayal cast long. In the midst of Quantum Innovations' rapid progress, Ladonna found herself facing not only external challenges but also a cunning adversary within the very walls of the company. Ladonna was determined to navigate it with strategic acumen, unwavering resolve, and the alliances she had worked so hard to build. The stakes were high, and the clash between Ladonna and Robert was about to reach a critical turning point that would test the limits of their wills and determination..

FIVE

J ustin Allen, the brilliant Manager of the Quantum Computer Project, had dedicated the last 10 years of his life to unlocking the potential of Quantum Computing. He had made significant breakthroughs but was still grappling with one persistent problem: the challenge of maintaining the stability of qubits temperature.

Qubits required extremely low temperatures to function, and this cooling process had been a significant obstacle. Justin had tried countless solutions over the years, but none had proven successful in keeping the qubits in superposition for extended periods.

Little did Justin know that Ladonna had been silently working on the very same problem for the past two years. Her project, aptly named "Stability of the Superposition," had led to a remarkable discovery that eliminated the need for cumbersome cooling processes. Moreover, Ladonna had been working on a prototype supercomputer and a system called OmniLink, which had the potential to revolutionize communication using quantum principles. Unknown to Justin she was using both prototypes and running a very sophisticated Quantum AI that was assisting her.

Meanwhile, Robert met his old college buddy Daniel at a posh downtown lounge. As they sipped expensive scotch, the conversation turned to Robert's ongoing efforts to undermine Ladonna.

"That woman has become a real thorn in my side," Robert fumed. "No matter what I try, she seems to counter me at every turn. I need to find her weaknesses, something I can exploit."

Daniel nodded thoughtfully. "A powerful woman like that must have skeletons somewhere. We just need to dig them up." He lowered his voice. "I may have a contact who can help access her classified records."

A slow smile spread across Robert's face. "I knew I could count on you, Daniel. Let's bury this Ladonna once and for all."

The day had arrived, and Ladonna's plan to bring Justin into her trust was set into motion. As Justin entered Ladonna's office, escorted by Jackson Reed, there was a sense of secrecy in the room. Ladonna and Lucy Wei, both seated in Ladonna's expansive office, awaited Justin's arrival. The room hummed with an electric energy, ready to witness the unveiling of Ladonna's breakthrough.

"Justin, thank you for joining us. Your dedication to the Quantum Computer Project has not gone unnoticed. I have been closely following your progress, and I must say that I am impressed with what you have been able to achieve."

"Mrs. Stone, your support means the world to me and the entire team. We have encountered challenges, especially with financing, but we remain steadfast in our pursuit of creating the first mass-production quantum computer." Justin explained.

"Justin, I want you to know that I share your dream. The creation of a Quantum Computer is not just a goal; it is a vision that I hold dear. The possibilities that lie ahead are outstanding."

"Mrs. Stone, forgive me for asking, but how do you plan to address the financial concerns surrounding the project?" "As I stated earlier, we have had some obstacles in the past."

Justin, when it comes to financing, I have strategies in mind. But before we discuss that further, I have one important matter to address. I believe we are about to embark on something groundbreaking, and with that comes the need for the utmost confidentiality. I would like you to sign this 'Non-Disclosure Agreement.'"

Lucy stood up and placed the NDA document in front of Justin. He picked it up, carefully read through its contents, and signed the document, sealing his commitment to secrecy.

"I understand the importance of confidentiality, Ms Wei, You have my word that I will uphold the terms of this NDA."

"Thank you, Justin. Now that we have established that, let us move forward. Mrs Stone has more to share."

"Yes Justin, you may not be aware of this but, I have been working on a solution to the qubit stability problem that has plagued us for years, and I think I have found the key."

"Mrs. Stone, you cannot be serious? I have tried everything, explored every avenue, and still, I have come up empty-handed. Could you really have found a solution?"

"Justin, I have dedicated countless hours to this research, and I believe I have discovered a breakthrough. The days of struggling with qubit stability are over. With your expertise and dedication, we can bring this vision to life."

"This is remarkable, Mrs. Stone! If what you are saying is true, it could revolutionize the entire field of Quantum Computing. The implications are enormous."

"Justin, with your commitment, we will turn this vision into a reality. Quantum Innovations will be at the forefront of a technological revolution, and together, we will unlock the true potential of Quantum Computing."

"I am ready, Mrs. Stone."

"Great, Justin. I would like you and Lucy to assemble your teams and ensure they all sign the NDA as well. We will meet in your laboratory this Friday, four days from now. At that time, we will assign personnel to their respective departments and begin the journey toward building the first fully functional general use Quantum Computer. Friday will mark the beginning of a new era. Together, we will achieve great strides for humanity."

As Justin left Ladonna's office, his mind raced with possibilities. He felt a renewed sense of purpose, fueled by Ladonna's support and the imminent collaboration of his teams. The stage was set, and Quantum Innovations was about to embark on a groundbreaking endeavor that would shape the future of technology.

Days turned into weeks, and weeks into months, as Ladonna and Justin pushed the boundaries of possibility. The lab hummed with activity, filled with the constant buzz of machinery and the chatter of their teams of resolute scientists and engineers. They worked tirelessly, often into the late hours of the night, refining the prototype, testing new algorithms, and ensuring the stability of the qubits.

In the depths of Quantum Innovations' secret lab, hidden from the prying eyes of competitors, Ladonna, Justin and Lucy saw the birth of their creation—a Quantum Computer that surpassed all expectations. Its sleek design housed an intricate network of qubits, aligned with precision, and capable of computations that were previously thought to be impossible.

Its immense computational power held the promise of transforming industries, from healthcare to finance, solving complex problems that classical computers could never tackle, and unlocking a new era of scientific exploration. The potential applications were limitless, from simulating molecular interactions for drug discovery to optimizing global logistics networks.

But there was more. Ladonna's OmniLink Communication device, a system that leveraged the principles of superposition and entanglement, was made even more efficient through the use of the Quantum Computer and the other brilliant minds in the lab. It worked beyond all expectations, allowing instantaneous and secure connections across vast distances. The OmniLink was not just a communication device; it was a symbol of a new age of connectivity, where information could be transmitted without the constraints of time and distance.

Over the next few months, they leveraged the power of the Quantum Computer to make even more advances at an astonishing pace. New algorithms were developed, efficiency was increased, and the once insurmountable problems of qubit stability were overcome. The team worked in perfect harmony, each member contributing their unique expertise to the project.

Together, Ladonna, Lucy, and Justin along with a teams of unparalleled talent and engineers had achieved the breakthrough of the millennium. Their secret project, Stability of the Superposition, was poised to change the course of history, solidifying Quantum Innovations' position as a leader in technological innovation. The world was about to witness a quantum leap in technology, one that would redefine the very fabric of reality.

The world held its breath in anticipation. The countdown had begun, and the future of technology was on the brink of a new era. The Quantum Computer and OmniLink were no longer dreams; they were realities, tangible manifestations of human ingenuity and perseverance.

The doors of the lab would soon open, and the world would be invited to gaze upon the marvels that had been created within its walls. The Quantum Computer and OmniLink were ready to reshape the world as we know it, heralding a future where the boundaries of possibility were expanded, and the horizons of human potential were broadened.

In the quiet moments, when the lab was still, and the machines were at rest, Ladonna would stand before their creation, a sense of awe and satisfaction washing over her. They had done it. They had taken the abstract principles of quantum mechanics and turned them into something real, something that would change the world.

The journey had been long and fraught with challenges, but they had emerged victorious. The legacy of Quantum Innovations was secure, and the future was bright, filled with the promise of discovery, innovation, and endless possibility.

SIX

Ladonna Stone sat in her office, viewing charts, data, and photographs of Quantum Innovations' key executives and board members. Her one-of-a-kind, state-of-the-art desk, with a display monitor built directly into it. The glass top, laser etched so that from her point of view, she could see a custom desktop displaying all the information, however, to anyone else sitting on the opposite side of the desk it would appear as dark tinted glass.

It was a crisp autumn day and Ladonna was deeply engrossed in her work. She was working with a custom AI she had developed herself named Aliah, named after her daughter. Aliah was not just an ordinary AI; she was a masterpiece of technology and innovation, developed using the prototype Quantum computer that Ladonna had created. Aliah possessed a vast array of capabilities that set her apart from any other AI in existence.

Aliah could replicate any voice or sound with remarkable accuracy, making her an exceptional tool for voice analysis and recognition. She could also generate highly convincing text for virtually any situation, a skill that Ladonna had honed to perfection for various purposes, including crafting persuasive messages and documents.

One of Aliah's many impressive features was her ability to continuously monitor her own systems for any signs of intrusion or breach.

If she detected any unauthorized access, her immediate response was to investigate the source with relentless determination. Aliah had been trained to seek out the hacker and extract as much information as possible from their digital trail. She would leave executable files to monitor the hacker's activities and gather valuable insights. Furthermore, Aliah was programmed to follow the data that she purposefully provided to the hacker, creating a trail that led back to the intruder's digital doorstep.

This intricate web of capabilities made Aliah an invaluable asset in Ladonna's quest to protect Quantum Innovations and uncover any potential threats or deception. As Ladonna delved deeper into her work, she knew that she could rely on Aliah to be her vigilant digital guardian, ensuring the company's security and integrity remained intact while unraveling the mysteries of power and ambition within the organization.

Meanwhile, a week earlier, Daniel had met with a hacker he had been in contact with to discuss penetrating Quantum's systems. The hacker claimed he could access Ladonna's personal files.

When the hack began, Aliah immediately detected it and allowed access to files she had been programed to provide. This granted Aliah backdoor access to the hacker's own systems. She fed the hacker fabricated records with that would appear real and genuine but were not. The purpose of these files were to tag anyone that was trying to hack into Quantum Innovations computers or Ladonna's personal computers and provide irrefutable proof of the identity of the hacker.

What Robert didn't know was that Aliah had detected the unauthorized access immediately. She allowed the hacker access to harmless files filled with false data that had telltale tags that were there to allow law enforcement to trace the intrusion directly to the hacker. Also, Aliah traced the intruder back to the source computer, activated cameras, and started recordings to identify the hacker, recorded all keystrokes and conversations. Aliah also tagged the data pulled by the hacker with a tracker that would copy the IP addresses, activate cameras, and start recordings on any other computer that was used to read the data even if the data was put on another hard drive or thumb stick, then send the information back to be stored in Ladonna's cloud server. All of this happened without alerting the hacker or the viewers of the data.

The false data showed doctored financial documents and emails that seemingly belonged to Ladonna. In reality, these were completely fabricated by Aliah.

Daniel retrieved the falsified records and excitedly brought them to Robert. "My hacker contact got into her systems," Daniel said. "I have all her personal files right here." "I hope this information can ruin her!"

When Daniel presented the ill-gotten records to Robert, Aliah was embedded in the files. As Robert eagerly plugged the flash drive into his laptop, hungry to uncover Ladonna's supposed misdeeds, he unknowingly granted Aliah access to his systems. Aliah immediately started to turn on the camera and microphone. She recorded all that was said and uploaded it to the cloud.

Robert was thrilled, not realizing the data was fake. Aliah monitored their conversation, gathering intel for Ladonna.

"I will look this all over. Let's keep this between us for now," Robert said, oblivious to Aliah's surveillance. He had taken the bait, falling right into Ladonna's trap.

Aliah compiled a detailed report with the hacker's IP address, location, photo, and transcript of Robert, and Daniel's discussion. She placed it in a folder marked as "What the Hack?" for Ladonna's review.

By allowing the hack, Aliah had outmaneuvered them. Ladonna would soon know of Robert and Daniel's deception thanks to Aliah's ingenious surveillance. The AI had enabled Ladonna to stay ahead in this dangerous game of power.

Barbara Hightower has been with Quantum Innovations for several years and has built a reputation for her strong organizational skills and attention to detail. She has a background in human resources and has been instrumental in managing employee relations, talent acquisition, and fostering a positive work culture within the company. Barbara's deep knowledge of the organization and its employees made her a valuable resource for Ladonna as she navigates the web of deceit and power struggles within Quantum Innovations.

Ladonna's sharp mind pieced together the puzzle, exposing the hidden motivations and agendas of those who held positions of influence. She saw through the façades, recognizing the intricate dance of power and ambition that governed Quantum Innovations. Ladonna called Barbara and requested the Personnel records she needed.

"Hello, Barbara, I would like you to send me the encrypted files for a few employees. I am emailing you the names now. Also, Barbara, I would like you to personally handle this, some of the files are of our key executives and board members." Ladonna wanted to know everything about their backgrounds, their alliances, and their past achievements. However, she did not inform Barbara of that.

"Right away, Mrs Stone!"

The encrypted email was within her inbox in minutes.

Ladonna compiled the information on everyone she wanted to investigate, creating dossiers for each. Aliah assisted her, cross-referencing information and drawing connections between individuals. The machine learning algorithms used historical data to predict new output values, enhancing her understanding of the network of power within Quantum Innovations.

"Now, let us start unraveling the threads of their connections," Ladonna thought to herself, filled with determination. As she sat down at her computer, she noticed that a new folder was in the top right-hand corner of her desktop. It was titled, What the Hack?, she immediately knew someone had been trying to access her digital information. She smiled, knowing the protocols she had built into Aliah for just this kind of thing. She opened the folder.

Meanwhile, at his lavish high-rise apartment, Robert eagerly accessed the files handed over by Daniel, a satisfied grin gracing his face as he believed he was delving into the pilfered records extracted from Ladonna's servers and hard drives. Aliah diligently observed his every action, systematically documenting his interactions with the fabricated data.

With unwavering confidence, Robert proclaimed, "Ladonna, you're within my grasp now. By the end of this month, I'll ascend to the position of CEO." His laughter reverberated through the room, an expression of his unbridled elation. Little did he realize that his jubilation only contributed to the growing trove of evidence that Ladonna had accumulated.

Over time, Robert carefully constructed alliances and cultivated a network of supporters. Nevertheless, Ladonna's relentless quest for truth, bolstered by Aliah's capabilities, was systematically dismantling the intricately crafted façade he had erected.

Even with just a cursory glance at the files gathered through Aliah's meticulous efforts, Ladonna gained a profound insight into the depths of Robert's ambitions and the extent to which he would go further his interests while undermining her own. Ladonna delved deeper into this intricate web of deception, she unveiled the layers of Robert's concealed motives and clandestine schemes. Aliah's advanced predictive algorithms became invaluable, unveiling intricate patterns and connections, exposing intertwined personal histories fueled by ambitions, loyalty dynamics, and the underlying driving forces.

Determined to unearth all the concealed truths lurking beneath the surface, Ladonna called upon Barbara to lend her expertise in arranging private meetings with each of the company's executives and board members. These personal conversations, coupled with the valuable insights provided by Aliah, proved essential in comprehending the genuine motivations and allegiances of Quantum Innovations' top leadership.

Over the next few days, Ladonna met with each executive and board member, engaging in insightful conversations that revealed more about their characters and intentions. Her custom AI continued to assist her, analyzing the data and providing her with valuable insights.

One by one, Ladonna exposed the missteps and manipulations of those aligned with Robert, effectively eroding their credibility within the company. Her strategic brilliance, combined with the power of machine learning, continued to shift the balance of power within Quantum Innovations.

The tension between Ladonna and Robert had been simmering beneath the surface for weeks. The situation reached a boiling point during a critical board meeting, attended by all key executives and board members, along with several department heads and team leaders. The meeting was meant to discuss the company's strategic direction, but it quickly became a battleground for control and influence.

Robert, feeling threatened by Ladonna's discreet investigation into his activities, decided to confront her openly. He sensed that she was closing in on his secrets, and he felt the need to challenge her authority.

Ladonna, on the other hand, was well aware of Robert's growing desperation. Her file marked, 'What the Hack?' kept growing and Roberts plans were laid bare.

She knew that he would try to confront her, and she was prepared to face him. Her secret weapon, Aliah, had provided her with insights into his strategies.

The exchange began when Robert openly questioned Ladonna's leadership during the meeting.

"Ladonna, your secretive actions and manipulations are not in the best interests of Quantum Innovations. What are you hiding? What is your hidden agenda?" Robert said coldly.

Ladonna, responding calmly but firmly: "Robert, my only agenda is the success and integrity of this company. I have nothing to hide. Can you say the same?"

Robert, growing more agitated: "I challenge your vision and your methods. You are leading us down a path that I cannot support."

Ladonna, maintaining her composure: "I appreciate your concerns, Robert, but I assure you that every decision I make is for the greater good of Quantum Innovations. Your resistance seems more personal than professional. Is there something specific you'd like to discuss?"

Robert, attempting to rally support: "I believe others in this room share my concerns. Your leadership is dividing this company."

Ladonna, with a decisive tone: "Robert, if you or anyone else has concerns, I am open to discussing them privately. But let's not mistake personal ambition for genuine concern for the company. I am committed to transparency, collaboration, and innovation. If you have evidence to the contrary, present it. Otherwise, let's move forward and focus on what truly matters."

The room fell into a stunned silence. Ladonna's clear and decisive response had effectively silenced Robert's accusations. The entire room was captivated by the clash of intellect and will, as the two leaders battled for control and influence.

Robert had believed that by challenging Ladonna openly, he could rally support from others in the company who might share his concerns. However, he had miscalculated Ladonna's resolve. Ladonna had understood that by facing Robert openly and decisively, she could demonstrate the strength of her resolve to the entire company.

The exchange ended and Ladonna had solidified her authority and vision for the company. The battle for control of Quantum Innovations had entered a new and more public phase, and both Ladonna and Robert knew that the coming weeks would be critical in determining the future of the company.

The room was left in a state of tense anticipation, with everyone aware that they had witnessed a significant turning point in the company's history.

As Ladonna continued her investigation, she discovered more encrypted messages and clandestine meetings, all pointing to Robert's betrayal. Aliah's machine learning algorithms helped her analyze the data, solidifying her resolve to bring him down.

In the meantime, Ladonna increased her security measures, ensuring that her breakthroughs and strategic plans remained hidden from prying eyes. The tension between her and Robert grew with each passing day, leading to fierce encounters and heated debates.

Ladonna's discreet sharing of her findings with her trusted allies, Lucy and Jackson, ensured that they were aware of the growing threat. Together, they strategized and planned their next move in this intricate game of power.

Ladonna was closing in, gathering the evidence needed to expose his betrayal and protect Quantum Innovations from further harm. The information unveiled a web of secrets, bringing Ladonna one step closer to unraveling the truth.

Aliah had become a vital tool in her investigation, allowing her to predict outcomes and analyze trends. Aliah, with her ability to learn and adapt, had become an essential part of her strategy, giving her an edge in the complex chess game of power within Quantum Innovations.

SEVEN

Sitting at her desk, looking at the display monitor, delving into the interconnections of events. With great care, she initiated an in-depth review of each file, cross-referencing details and weaving links among individuals. Aliah assisted her in mapping out a network of power. She identified those who supported Robert Westfield and those who remained neutral or potentially aligned with her.

Robert had built alliances and garnered support, passionately believing he was the rightful heir to the CEO throne. However, Ladonna's relentless pursuit of the truth would unravel his carefully constructed facade.

Ladonna continued to unearth a labyrinth of hidden agendas that extended far beyond Robert's machinations. It became evident that some executives and board members had personal histories intertwined with their ambitions, shaping their loyalties, and driving their motivations.

Determined to uncover the secrets lurking beneath the surface, Ladonna called Barbara, the human resources manager at Quantum Innovations, to assist her in this delicate endeavor.

"Barbara, I would like you to set up meetings with each executive and board member separately," Ladonna instructed Barbara over the phone. Her voice was firm and resolute. "I want to have personal conversations with them, to gain insight into their perspectives in their divisions."

Barbara, recognizing the gravity of the situation, responded with unwavering commitment. "Consider it done, Mrs. Stone. I will schedule the meetings and ensure all the necessary arrangements are in place."

With Barbara's support, Ladonna knew she was one step closer to unraveling the intricate tapestry of deception that threatened to undermine the stability of Quantum Innovations. The personal conversations she would have with each executive and board member would be the key to understanding their true motivations and allegiances.

As Ladonna hung up the phone, her mind was filled with anticipation. She knew that within the confines of those conversations lay the secrets that would expose the hidden alliances and ultimately determine the course of her battle against Robert. Ladonna's determination became sterner than ever as she prepared to embark on this critical phase of her plan.

Over the next few days, Ladonna met with each executive and board member, engaging in insightful conversations that revealed more about their characters and intentions. She skillfully probed their histories and motivations, carefully extracting the information she needed to dismantle Robert's network of supporters.

In these encounters, Ladonna uncovered stories of betrayal, personal ambitions, and hidden loyalties. She listened attentively, using her intuition and intellect to separate fact from fiction, determining who could be swayed to her side and who posed the greatest threats to her vision for Quantum Innovations.

One by one, Ladonna exposed the missteps and manipulations of those aligned with Robert, effectively eroding their credibility within the company. She used her knowledge of their weaknesses to weaken their alliances and exploit the divisions that had been concealed beneath the surface.

Ladonna sat across from Mr. Johnson, a key executive whose loyalty seemed to lie firmly with Robert Westfield. As she sought to sway his allegiance, Ladonna understood the importance of maintaining her integrity and avoiding underhanded tactics. She needed to find a way to make Mr. Johnson question his support for Robert.

"Mr. Johnson, I appreciate your dedication and commitment to Robert. However, I believe it is essential to consider all aspects before making a final decision. Quantum Innovations requires a leader who values transparency, collaboration, and innovation. Allow me to share with you a broader perspective. In my experience, a leader's character and integrity play a crucial role in shaping the company's culture and success. I invite you to reflect on the qualities you value in a leader and consider whether they align with Robert's actions and decision-making."

"I have always admired Robert's ambition and strategic thinking. Nevertheless, you are right. Character is vital in a leader. Can you give me an example of how your leadership differs from his?"

"Certainly, Mr. Johnson. While I believe in healthy competition and driving the company forward, I also prioritize fostering a collaborative and inclusive environment. I value the ideas and contributions of every individual within our organization, regardless of their position or tenure. My approach to leadership is rooted in empowering our teams, encouraging open communication, and embracing innovation. By embracing diverse perspectives and nurturing an atmosphere of trust and respect, we can unlock the full potential of Quantum Innovations and drive it to new heights."

Mr. Johnson pondered Ladonna's words, considering the stark contrast between her leadership style and the potentially cut-throat tactics he had witnessed from Robert.

"Ladonna, your vision for Quantum Innovations is compelling, and I appreciate your emphasis on collaboration and inclusiveness. I had not fully considered the impact of a leader's character on the overall success of the company. I will reassess my support for Robert and take your words into serious consideration."

"Thank you, Mr. Johnson. I value your thoughtful consideration, and I believe that together, we can build a stronger future for Quantum Innovations. Your support would be instrumental in driving positive change within our organization."

Their conversation continued, exploring the potential for growth and transformation under Ladonna's leadership. The subtle approach and genuine exchange of ideas had opened a door of possibility, allowing Ladonna to make progress in her mission to uncover Robert's true intentions and gain the support she needed.

Ladonna's ability to expose the truth and cast doubt on Robert's credibility began to shift the balance of power within Quantum Innovations. Her strategic brilliance was a force to be reckoned with, and Robert sensed the threat she posed.

Robert, relaxed in his usual manner but seething with indignation, confronted Ladonna in a heated exchange. Their clash of intellectualism and the battle of wits unfolded before the entire company. However, at this time Ladonna had already uncovered several illegal acts Robert had already committed and was still collecting information.

"Ladonna, you may think you are clever, but you underestimate my influence and the loyalty of those who support me. You won't succeed in dismantling my network."

"Robert, your web of deceit is unraveling. The divisions within the company are becoming clearer, and the truth will prevail. I won't let your manipulations taint the future of Quantum Innovations."

The tension between Ladonna and Robert escalated, with each move they made in the complex chess game of power carrying weight and consequence. Ladonna anticipated Robert's every move, staying steps ahead of him, and revealing his missteps to those who had once aligned with him.

As Ladonna dove into her investigation, she could not shake off a growing suspicion about Robert Westfield, the seasoned executive, who had harbored resentment toward her appointment as CEO. There was something about his demeanor that undermined her authority and worked behind the scenes, which set off alarm bells in her mind. How deeply did his deceit go?

Ladonna discreetly probed deeper into Robert's activities, gathering fragments of information that hinted at a darker agenda. She analyzed financial records, scrutinized email exchanges, and consulted with her trusted confidantes: Lucy Wei and Jackson Reed. Her state-of-the-art computer allowed her to access her custom desktop, showing all the computer information she needed. The dark tinted glass concealed her actions from anyone else in the room, ensuring that her investigation remained a secret.

One evening, as Ladonna reviewed a confidential report, a pattern began to emerge. As she already was aware, Robert had been communicating with an individual from a rival company, Daniel, exchanging information that seemed too strategic to be coincidental. This realization had filled her with anger and determination to expose Robert as the fraud he was.

She continued her investigation, determined to confirm her suspicions before making any move. Ladonna knew that exposing Robert's betrayal would require even more evidence and she carefully crafted a plan. She reached out to her contacts in the intelligence community, leveraging her connections to gather discreet information about Robert's recent activities and to get guidance on what to do with the evidence she had already garnered.

Slowly and surely, the pieces of the puzzle fell into place. Ladonna discovered encrypted messages and clandestine meetings, all pointing to Robert's involvement in sharing Quantum Innovations' sensitive information with their competitor. The evidence confirmed her initial suspicion, solidifying her resolve to bring him down.

However, Ladonna understood the importance of timing. She could not afford to make a hasty move without being fully prepared. She continued to play the role of the unsuspecting CEO, observing Robert's every move, silently gathering the ammunition she needed to expose his treachery.

In the meantime, she continued to monitor the security measures she had put in place for weaknesses, ensuring that her breakthroughs and strategic plans remained undiscovered. She knew that her vision for Quantum Innovations was at stake, and she could not allow Robert's actions to sabotage their progress. The tension between Ladonna and Robert grew with each passing day. A simmering undercurrent of animosity and suspicion. They engaged in heated debates during executive meetings; their clashes of intellect and opposing visions created sparks that flew across the boardroom.

Ladonna's encounters with Robert became fierce and fiery, and every word and gesture held significance. She observed his condescending demeanor and the veiled arrogance that emanated from him, further confirming her belief in his duplicity. Ladonna discreetly kept Lucy and Jackson informed, ensuring they were aware of the growing threat.

EIGHT

Ladonna's relentless pursuit of the truth led her deeper into the labyrinth of deceit within Quantum Innovations. Her suspicions about Robert's collaboration with a rival company continued to grow, fueled by the evidence she had uncovered. Each new revelation painted a more damning picture, further solidifying her resolve to expose his treachery.

Ladonna maintained her cool demeanor, concealing her knowledge of Robert's betrayal. She knew that revealing things too soon could jeopardize her plan. Instead, she played the role of the inquisitive CEO, engaging Robert in conversations that would subtly extract information while keeping her true intentions concealed.

One evening, after a long day of executive meetings, Ladonna found herself alone in her office, contemplating her next move. She reviewed the latest batch of documents she had acquired, scrutinizing every word, and analyzing every connection. As the pieces fell into place, a clearer picture emerged.

Ladonna: (muttering to herself) "If Robert thinks he can get away with sharing our secrets for personal gain, he is gravely mistaken. I won't let him sabotage Quantum Innovations."

One by one, Ladonna gained the support of those who had fallen victim to Robert's manipulation. She united them under a shared purpose: to safeguard the company and ensure that its secrets remained secure. As the circle of trust grew, Ladonna's confidence in her ability to dismantle Robert's network of supporters solidified. She strategically positioned her allies within key positions of influence, eroding Robert's power base from within.

Amidst this covert operation, Aliah had continue to follow the data, listening to Robert's plans. Robert had inadvertently provided Ladonna a hidden communication channel used by Robert and his accomplices. The contents of the messages sent shockwaves to her spine. The messages revealed the extent of Robert's betrayal. She saw his plans, his collaborations with a rival company, and their intent to exploit Quantum Innovations for profit.

"So, this is what you've been up to, Robert. You thought you could get away with it, but I see through your deceit," she thought to herself.

With the final piece of the puzzle in place, Ladonna prepared to make her move. She knew that the battle against Robert and his collaborators had reached a critical juncture. The time for subtle maneuvers had ended. The stage was set for the ultimate confrontation, where the fate of Quantum Innovations would be decided.

With unwavering determination, she was poised to cast a brilliant light into the shadows that had long concealed the inner workings of the company. Her intent was clear: to unravel the intricate web of deceit meticulously woven by Robert and safeguard the future of Quantum Innovations. The wealth of information she had unearthed about Robert was substantial, yet she yearned for more. A meticulous plan began to take shape.

NINE

Ladonna's mind was made up as she devised a plan to expose Robert's deceit. She understood that catching him in the act was crucial to dismantling his network of collaborators and securing Quantum Innovations' future. With unwavering determination, she set her intricate trap in motion. Ladonna created a dummy project, one that was touted to be revolutionary—a technological marvel that would disrupt the industry. She carefully crafted the illusion, ensuring every detail was convincing. The project plans, stored safely in her office safe, held the key to luring Robert into her web of deception.

As the rumours of the groundbreaking project began to circulate within Quantum Innovations, Ladonna observed Robert's reactions closely. She watched for signs that he was taking the bait, waiting for the right moment to strike. Days turned into weeks, and the tension within the company grew. Ladonna allowed the information to leak slowly, ensuring it reached the ears of Robert and his accomplices. The excitement surrounding the project intensified, igniting a fierce sense of competition and curiosity among the employees.

One evening, Ladonna was in her office, reviewing the progress of her plans thus far. The door creaked open, and Robert entered, with a face covered in curiosity and disdain.

"Ladonna, I could not help but hear about this revolutionary project you are working on. Care to share details with me?"

"Robert, always eager to know what is happening, aren't you? I am afraid the details of the project are strictly confidential. You will have to wait like everyone else."

"Well, Ladonna, I hope this project lives up to the hype? We would not want it to be another empty promise like some of your previous initiatives."

"Rest assured, Robert, this project will deliver beyond expectations. You will have to be patient just like everyone else."

Robert's attempt to rattle Ladonna only fueled her determination. She knew that he was growing increasingly desperate to get his hands on the project plans; he was eager to exploit them for personal gain. The trap was set, and she was confident that he would take the bait.

As the days elapsed, Ladonna meticulously monitored Robert's actions. She noticed subtle changes in his behavior: secretive conversations, furtive glances, and unexplained absences from his usual duties. It became clear to her that he was actively working with the rival company, sharing Quantum Innovations' secrets.

Ladonna continued to play her role as the CEO who held the key to the project's success. She maintained a facade of confidence, allowing Robert to believe that he was one step ahead. Little did he know that every move he made was being carefully documented, evidence that would seal his fate.

After she read a message from Jackson, Ladonna knew that it was about time to bring Robert to the light. He has to be exposed. The message read, "Robert is on his way to your office. I am in position."

Ladonna had to prepare for Robert's visit to her office. She arranged the plans in her safe meticulously ensuring that the fake ones, indistinguishable from the real ones without thorough examination, were placed in a prominent position. She knew that Robert's greed and eagerness to seize the plans would cloud his judgement.

Robert arrived at her office. He wore confidence in a proud way that was palpable, but little did he know that he was walking into a trap carefully orchestrated by the woman he sought to undermine and destroy.

"Ah, Ladonna," Robert greeted her with false congeniality. "I hope I am not interrupting anything important?"

"Not at all, Robert. I was just finishing up some work. Please, have a seat."

As Robert settled into the chair across from her desk, Ladonna saw the motive on his face. It was the perfect moment for the plan to unfold. Just as Ladonna was about to lock her safe, Jackson Reed entered her office in a rush, a look of urgency on his face.

"Ladonna, I am sorry to interrupt, but we have an urgent security matter that requires your immediate attention."

Immediately, Ladonna shifted her attention from the safe to Robert. She turned to him and said,

"I am terribly sorry, Robert. It seems I must attend to this matter urgently. Please, forgive the interruption."

Robert waved a dismissive hand, a hint of annoyance in his expression. "No problem at all, Ladonna, I understand. We can continue our discussion another time."

As Ladonna hurriedly left the office with Jackson, she intentionally left the safe ajar. The fake plans were there and visible for Robert to see.

Fortunately, Robert saw the opportunity. He approached the safe feeling excited and hungry to destroy Ladonna. His greed and ambition blinded any caution he might have had, and he quickly pulled out his phone, took pictures of the supposed valuable plans.

With the evidence captured, Robert carefully returned the plans to their original position in the safe. His heart pounded with anxiety. He hoped no one saw his move. He became optimistic about his desire to oust Ladonna. Sadly, he was foolish not to see that he was already a pawn. Just as Robert returned to his position, Ladonna came back, "Crysis averted." She said to Robert. "Apologies for the sudden interruption. I appreciate your understanding. We will continue our discussion at another time, as you suggested."

Robert replied, "Of course, Ladonna. We can pick up where we left off on another day. I look forward to that."

The trap had sprung, and he had unknowingly fallen right into it. Ladonna's calculated move had brought her one step closer to exposing his true intentions and securing the future of Quantum Innovations.

As Ladonna and Robert exchanged pleasantries, their words held deeper meanings, concealed within the layers of their conversation. The battle for power and control had escalated, and the stage was set for a showdown that would determine the fate of both individuals and the company they represented.

Later that evening, Ladonna received an urgent message from Jackson Reed, who had been monitoring the communication channels used by Robert and his accomplices. The message contained a conversation that left no doubt about their intentions.

"Ladonna, I have intercepted a message. Robert and his accomplice from the rival company are planning to meet. They are discussing the project plans and their strategy for exploiting them." Said Jackson.

"Well done, Jackson. We have the evidence we need. Prepare a file with all the intercepted communications. It is time to bring Robert's treachery into the light."

Ladonna's determination swelled within her. She stood ready to expose Robert's collusion with Marshall Industries and to ensure that justice prevailed. The trap had been set, and the intricate chess game of power within Quantum Innovations was poised for a dramatic conclusion — one that would push the boundaries of loyalty, integrity, and the depths to which people would go to safeguard their ambitions.

It had been a demanding week, but the promise of the weekend beckoned. Ladonna eagerly anticipated the moments ahead. She knew that Michael would be departing for his climbing trip with friends and business associates on Saturday, and the prospect of reuniting with him and her children warmed her heart. As she settled into her SUV, the engine roared to life, and the soothing notes of jazz filled the air from her playlist. She craved a moment of relaxation. The challenges with Robert awaited her on Monday, and all she wanted now was to reach the sanctuary of her home.

Upon arriving, she pulled into the long driveway and into the welcoming embrace of the temperature-controlled garage. Switching off the engine, she sat there for a moment, savoring the final strains of the melody. As the music concluded, she stepped out of the car and made her way into the house.

In the kitchen, Michael was busy experimenting with a new recipe, a warm smile on his face as he sensed Ladonna's arrival. He moved towards her, enveloping her in a tender, loving hug. "Hello, my love. Welcome home! I hope you had a fruitful day at work."

Ladonna, feeling the stresses of the day begin to melt away, replied softly, "Everything I do, I do for you and my babies." She looked into his caring eyes and was rewarded with a gentle kiss — a silent acknowledgment of their unspoken understanding. "Your babies are growing into wonderful teens." he playfully replied.

"Where are my babies?" she inquired just as playfully, her maternal instincts yearning to embrace their children.

Michael explained that they were engrossed in a movie but assured her that the interruption of their mother would be most welcome. As she headed towards the theater room, Ladonna paused for a moment, thoughts of Monday and the impending events flickering through her mind. With a determined sigh, she cleared her thoughts and entered the room with boundless joy.

TEN

The room was clouded with expectation as the board members took their seats. Ladonna could feel the weight of the moment, the future of Quantum Innovations hanging in the balance. With a steady breath, she rose from her seat, the real OmniLink plans securely tucked away in the Quantum lab's safe.

Ladonna: "Good morning, esteemed board members. Today, I stand before you to introduce a project that will change the landscape of communication forever. I present to you OmniLink, a revolutionary technological breakthrough that will redefine how we connect with the world."

Ladonna's voice reverberated with a fiery passion that filled every corner of the room as she continued to unveil the remarkable potential of OmniLink. It was a moment she had been waiting for, a culmination of her relentless pursuit of excellence and her unyielding belief in the power of innovation. This project was more than just a professional endeavor—it was a labor of love that had consumed her thoughts and fueled her determination for years prior to becoming the CEO of Quantum Innovations.

With each word she spoke, Ladonna's passion ignited the hearts and minds of the board members. They could feel her unwavering conviction, her unwavering commitment to pushing the boundaries of what was possible. She had taken the initiative to explore uncharted territories, venturing into the realm of revolutionizing communication. Ladonna had seen the limitations of existing technologies, and it was her relentless pursuit of progress that had driven her to push the boundaries further.

Suddenly, Robert's rude interruption was heard.

Robert's voice echoed through the room, laced with anger and disbelief.

"Ladonna, I can't believe what I'm hearing! How can you possibly claim credit for something that rightfully belongs to Marshall Industries? They just issued a press release, boasting about their years of hard work and the imminent release of their groundbreaking project with the same name. Are you attempting to deceive us all?"

Ladonna's eyes narrowed; her voice filled with a calm determination. She had anticipated Robert's outburst and addressed his accusations head on.

"Robert, I understand your skepticism and your motivation for it. But what if I told you that the information you received about Marshall Industries was, in fact, part of my plan?"

Confusion swept through the room as Robert's confident facade wavered for a moment. The other board members leaned in, eager to hear Ladonna's response.

"What did you mean, Ladonna?" Ladonna looked around the room at the members present. "Please bear with me, I have something I am sure you will be very interested in." Then she turned her attention back to Robert.

"I mean that I have been well aware of your collaboration with Marshall Industries for quite some time. I have evidence that you have been sharing Quantum Innovations' trade secrets for personal gain."

Ladonna glanced at Jackson, who stood nearby, monitoring the room. His surveillance equipment had captured the truth.

"Jackson, it is time." She exclaimed.

Jackson stepped forward, holding a tablet in his hand. With the press of a button, a video began playing on the screen, capturing the attention of everyone present. On the screen, Robert was seen approaching Ladonna's open safe with a mix of eagerness and caution. His eyes scanned the contents, settling on the alluring project plans that appeared to hold great value. With a deft hand, he reached inside and extracted the plans, handling them with care.

A sinister smile flickered across Robert's face as he took out his phone and took pictures of crucial information within the stolen documents. Painstakingly, he snapped each page, ensuring that he captured every detail and critical piece of information. The video recorded his calculated movements, capturing the evidence that would expose his true intentions. After meticulously taking pictures of the plans, Robert returned them to their original position in the safe, concealing any trace of his intrusion. He stepped back, feeling satisfied and unaware of all the missing critical components and data.

As the video footage continued, a new location appeared, transitioning to a dark and ominous parking lot. The old church parking lot was shrouded in darkness, a perfect backdrop for their clandestine conversations. Robert and Daniel, a top executive from Marshall Industries, his old college friend turned sinister accomplice.

Their conversation unfolded in hushed tones. The words spelled out harmful plans and strategies. The secret meeting revealed the depths of their collaboration, an insidious pact forged to collapse Quantum Innovations' new CEO. Their voices carried the weight of whispered conspiracies, plotting the downfall of Ladonna and everything she had fought to build.

Robert gazed fondly at his old friend. "Daniel, can you believe it's been 15 years since we started these secret rendezvous? We were just ambitious kids back then, dreaming of making it big. Now look how far we've come."

Daniel chuckled, pride glinting in his eyes. "Our partnership has certainly proven fruitful over the years. We've built quite the corporate empire for ourselves. But I suspect you called me out here for more than just nostalgia. What new scheme have you been cooking up in that devious mind of yours?"

Robert's eyes twinkled mischievously. "You always could read me like a book. Let's just say I recently acquired some intel that could grant us unlimited power and influence beyond our wildest dreams."

Daniel raised an intrigued eyebrow. "Do tell. You know I love the thrill of a high-stakes corporate coup. How exactly do you propose we secure this power?"

"My friend, Quantum Innovations is secretly developing a revolutionary communication system called OmniLink," Robert continued, his excitement growing. "I managed to get an advance peek at the ultra-top-secret plans outlining the technology. It would enable instantaneous, unhackable data transmission globally. We're talking about controlling the future of communication itself!"

Daniel let out an impressed whistle. "Now that would be quite a game-changing coup! Global telecoms would pay any price to license this technology. We could license the tech and be billionaires overnight. "We would gain a virtual monopoly. But why come to me first? I'm sure you could broker a king's ransom for this with our competitors."

Robert leaned in, glancing around furtively as if even the trees had ears. "An outside party did approach me, a woman of, shall we say, questionable motives? Offered an exorbitant sum that made my eyes pop. But you and I go way back. Our partnership predates all else. I wanted to extend you the courtesy of first bid."

Daniel clasped Robert's shoulder appreciatively. "I won't forget this. With OmniLink, we control the future of communication itself. The entire telecom sector would be beholden to us. We'll be masters of the universe!" How did you get your hands on such closely guarded plans?"

Robert shrugged nonchalantly. "I have my methods. But imagine being able to transmit huge datasets across massive distances instantly without lag or interruption. This tech could reshape society as we know it. And I intend for us to be the ones controlling the reins."

Daniel's eyes glinted hungrily. "To wield that kind of power over information and connectivity...we'd effectively control the modern world! Governments, corporations, financial markets - all would kneel at our feet. We could name our price!"

He gripped Robert's shoulder, mind racing. "My friend, this is it - our golden ticket, the big one we've been waiting for. No more nickel and diming. But we must act strategically to capitalize on this. I assume you have a plan?"

Robert grinned wolfishly. "My man, I'm always ten steps ahead. Here's what I'm thinking..."

As Robert outlined his scheme, Daniel listened raptly, interrupting occasionally to suggest modifications or contingency options. The air crackled with electric ambition as two cunning minds fine-tuned their plot.

"Brilliant, positively diabolical!" Daniel exclaimed after hearing the details. "This OmniLink coup will launch us straight into the billionaires club. Not to mention getting you your well deserve job as CEO. Ladonna will not know what hit her." He laughed. Man, Marshall Industries had better have my name on a corner office!"

"With OmniLink's global domination, we can handpick our extravagant corner suites atop any shiny skyscraper we desire," Robert chuckled. This should destroy Ladonna. I cannot wait. "I'll fly you out once I've seized control. You concentrate on leveraging Marshall Tech's resources to maximize our gains."

Daniel shook Robert's hand vigorously. "The game is afoot my friend! Our empire awaits."

As the two scheming masterminds parted ways, both could barely contain their glee, intoxicated by the fantasy of unlimited power and prestige soon to be theirs. The promise of OmniLink had opened the floodgates to their deepest desires. Lofty ambitions now seemed within grasp, a mere steppingstone to their planned empire of unrivaled wealth and control. Egos swollen with delusions of grandeur.

The video ended, the room remained silent, the weight of Robert's betrayal hanging in the air. The revelations had shattered the trust that had once existed, leaving a sense of uncertainty and a need for justice.

Ladonna's gaze hardened, her voice firm.

"Robert, your actions have consequences. Betrayal of this magnitude cannot go unpunished."

"Gentlemen and ladies, what you have just witnessed is undeniable proof of Robert's duplicity. He has not only betrayed our trust but also jeopardized the future of Quantum Innovations. But fear not, for the wheels of justice are already turning. The FBI has been alerted, and they are launching an investigation into corporate espionage and theft of intellectual property."

"Robert, your actions will have severe consequences, not just for yourself, but for your friend Daniel and Marshall Industries as well."

Robert's face contorted with rage and desperation; his confident demeanor shattered. The truth had been laid bare before him, leaving him exposed and without escape.

Agents of the FBI had been sitting in the corner of the room monitoring the entire exchange. They swiftly apprehended Robert, leading him out of the room amidst his protests of innocence, Ladonna handed them a copy of the video that also included the information recovered after the hack and returned to her seat. The weight of the moment settled upon her, and she felt relieved of the threat Robert posed.

The room buzzed with a mix of emotions— shock, anger, and uncertainty. The unveiling of truth had set in motion a series of events that would shape the destiny of Quantum Innovations, and everyone involved.

Whispers and murmurs filled the room as the board members grappled with the implications of Robert's betrayal. Ladonna's eyes scanned their faces, observing the mixture of disbelief and concern. She knew that the path ahead would be challenging, but she was determined to steer Quantum Innovations through this storm.

Ladonna's voice rang out with a tinge of sorrow, but her determination remained unyielding.

"I am deeply sorry that it has come to this, that one of our own has betrayed the trust we placed in him. Robert has been taking the hard work and innovations of our talented engineers and selling them to others. It is a grave offense, and he will face the consequences of his actions. But despite this setback, we must carry on with our mission. There is still much to cover, and I want to assure you that Quantum Innovations remains committed to delivering on our promises."

Ladonna's words resonated throughout the room, a testament to her resilience and leadership. The atmosphere shifted, as the focus shifted from Robert's betrayal to the future that awaited Quantum Innovations.

Ladonna's voice filled with strength and conviction.

"Now, let us continue with the presentation. After the presentation, a demonstration of OmniLink has been set up, and it will showcase the immense potential of this groundbreaking technology. We have worked tirelessly to perfect it, and today, you will witness firsthand how it will revolutionize communication and connectivity."

Glancing over at Justin Allen, the manager of the Quantum Computer Research Lab, trusted colleague, and brilliant engineer, Ladonna's eyes sparkled with a mixture of pride and gratitude. She explained to the board members that after assuming the role of CEO at Quantum Innovations, she had presented her audacious idea to Justin and his team. Together, they embarked on an extraordinary journey, fueled by a shared passion for innovation and a deep-rooted belief in the power of human ingenuity.

The room was again captivated by Ladonna's infectious energy and her unwavering determination. As she delved deeper into the story of OmniLink's inception, the audience could sense the magnitude of her dedication. This project had become an extension of her very being, a testament to her unyielding pursuit of excellence. Ladonna had poured her heart and soul into this endeavor, leaving no stone unturned in her quest for innovation.

Her voice resonated with an indomitable spirit, carrying the weight of countless hours spent brainstorming, researching, and refining. It was a journey marked by sleepless nights and tireless efforts, fueled by the belief that there was a better way to connect with the world.

As Ladonna painted a vivid picture of the challenges they had faced and the triumphs they had celebrated, her passion enveloped the room like a roaring flame. She explained how they dedicated countless hours, sacrificing their personal lives and pouring their hearts and souls into the development of OmniLink. Ladonna's leadership and vision guided the team through the ups and downs of the creative process. They overcame countless obstacles, pushing the boundaries of innovation to perfect the technology.

The board members could feel the intensity of her drive, her unwavering commitment to pushing these boundaries of what was deemed possible. It was a testament to the power of human imagination, Ladonna's intellect, and the relentless pursuit of progress.

With each word, Ladonna's voice became more impassioned, her gestures more animated. Her eyes sparkled with a fire that burned brighter with every passing moment. She was not simply presenting a project— she was unveiling a vision, a dream that had blossomed from the depths of her soul.

At that moment, they became believers. They understood why Mr. Cline had passionately pressed for her to be the CEO. They saw Ladonna's passion, her unwavering conviction, the scale of her unmatched intellect, and they couldn't help but be swept away by the magnitude of it. It was a transformative moment, a turning point that would redefine their understanding of what was possible.

With a heart filled with gratitude and a spirit brimming with passion, Ladonna knew that her journey had only just begun. This project, born out of love and nurtured with unwavering dedication, would become her legacy—a testament to the power of dreaming big and daring to defy the status quo. Together with her team, she would forge ahead, propelled by the unwavering belief that they could reshape the world.

The culmination of their efforts resulted in the creation of three functional prototypes—deployed via satellites over various areas around the world. These prototypes acted as beacons of possibility, showcasing the immense potential of OmniLink.

The satellites had already garnered attention from industry experts. It captured the imagination of engineers and technology enthusiasts wanting to know what the newly launched satellites were for.

The prototypes thrived in their own ecosystem, serving as a testament to the scalability and adaptability of OmniLink. Through its seamless integration into existing infrastructure, it demonstrated the potential for widespread adoption and transformation.

Ladonna shared the stories of a large business that had been a test market under strict guidance from the engineering team and ironclad NDAs had already seen unprecedented benefits from the early implementation of OmniLink. She highlighted internal case studies, showcasing how this technology would revolutionize communication and connectivity across all sectors. The impact would be tangible, transcending geographical barriers and fostering unprecedented collaboration.

As she unveiled the remarkable features and capabilities of OmniLink, Ladonna's enthusiasm was contagious. The room buzzed with anticipation, each board member envisioning the possibilities that lay ahead.

Ladonna's voice echoed with pride as she continued, "We are on the precipice of a new era, where communication is seamless, efficient, and limitless. OmniLink has the power to transform industries, connect communities, and bridge the gaps that have held us back for far too long. It is not just a product—it is a catalyst for change, an instrument of progress."

She paused for a moment, allowing her words to sink in. The room was filled with palpable energy, a shared belief in the transformative nature of OmniLink.

With unwavering determination, Ladonna concluded the introduction of her presentation, "Together, we have the opportunity to shape the future. Let us embrace this journey, fueled by innovation, collaboration, and the unwavering belief in the power of technology to unlock endless possibilities."

The room erupted in applause, excitement and optimism filling the air. The board members were captivated by Ladonna's vision, inspired by her dedication and the remarkable progress they had witnessed.

Ladonna had not only unveiled the brilliance of OmniLink but also shared the incredible journey that led to its creation. Her leadership and relentless pursuit of excellence had brought them to this moment—a moment that held the promise of revolutionizing the way humanity communicated.

As the applause subsided, Ladonna knew that this was just the beginning. The path ahead would be filled with challenges, but she had confidence in the capabilities of her team and the transformative power of OmniLink. Together, they would continue to push the boundaries, pushing the world closer to a future where connectivity knew no limits.

With a sly smile playing at the corners of her lips, Ladonna beckoned everyone to follow her to the grand auditorium where the demonstration would take place. The room buzzed with anticipation as the audience eagerly followed her lead, and took their seats, their curiosity piqued by the promise of a revelation that would leave them breathless.

Jackson Reed and his vigilant security team formed a protective perimeter, ensuring that the outside world would not intrude upon this momentous occasion. Their presence instilled a sense of confidence and reassurance, allowing Ladonna and her team to focus on the task at hand.

As the doors to the auditorium swung open, revealing the grandeur of the space, Ladonna stood at the center with her commanding presence radiating across the room. The audience settled into their seats, their eyes fixed on Ladonna, ready to witness the unveiling of Quantum Innovations' newest creation.

Years of tireless effort and unwavering dedication had led to this pivotal moment. The time had come to reveal one of the company's most groundbreaking and long-awaited products—a culmination of countless hours of innovation and ingenuity. The room fell into a hushed silence, the air pregnant with anticipation.

Among the attendees, Mr. Cline, the former CEO, took his assigned seat, alongside Quantum Innovations' ranking executives and the board. Still filled with shock and disbelief over the irrefutable proof of Robert's theft and collaboration with Marshall Industries, they were eager to see the fruits of Ladonna's labor.

"Ladies and gentlemen, I want to assure you that the future of Quantum Innovations remains bright. Much brighter than you can imagine," Ladonna began, her voice exuding confidence. "If you will indulge me, let us not forget the reasons we are gathered here today. The Quantum OmniLink is not just an idea; it is a reality."

Her words hung in the air, electrifying the atmosphere with excitement. The audience leaned in, eager to hear more about this revolutionary technology that would redefine connectivity and propel the world into a new era.

"I present to you the culmination of years of innovation, research, and dedication," Ladonna continued, her voice filled with conviction. "The OmniLink is designed to transcend barriers, bridge distances, and redefine connectivity. Ladies and gentlemen, the world is about to change."

As her words settled upon the audience, Ladonna's eyes gleamed with a mix of pride and anticipation. The moment had arrived to unveil the OmniLink Hub—a technological marvel powered by their state-of-the-art AI algorithm that transcended the limitations of traditional communication networks, rendering 4G and 5G technologies obsolete.

"With the Quantum OmniLink, buffering, data transmission delays, and dropped calls will be a thing of the past," Ladonna proclaimed, her voice brimming with excitement. "This communication hub creates a connection that remains unbroken unless the user intentionally turns it off. It provides unprecedented security and has security features that are aimed at discouraging hacking. Once someone starts to attempt a hack to any of the devices attached to OmniLink, an extremely efficient AI will track the hacker, retrieve all the relevant data from their computer, modem, and router and then contact law enforcement nearest to the hacker. Providing them with the hacker's location, a photo if there is a camera, and evidence they had attempted the hack. It provides these measures to all connected devices, also, it can connect to smartphones and tablets, smart home devices, and IoT devices, simulating any signal identity while delivering the maximum speed the connected device can produce.

A wave of awe swept through the audience, their murmurs of excitement echoing Ladonna's sentiments. The Quantum OmniLink had the power to revolutionize the way people communicate, breaking down barriers and connecting individuals across vast distances.

"The true marvel of the OmniLink lies in its speed and capacity," Ladonna continued, her voice tinged with admiration. "Each OmniLink node can seamlessly connect billions of devices, enabling uninterrupted communication and data transmission. Just imagine, a single OmniLink node could effortlessly handle the communication needs of North and South America and the related islands, that is millions of square miles without any drops in calls or data. We estimate that with three nodes, we can cover the entire globe."

The transmission power of the Quantum OmniLink left the audience in awe. Ladonna's voice grew even stronger, brimming with unwavering conviction.

"It is capable of transmitting billions of petabytes of data per attosecond. All communication will be instant, seamless, and reliable," Ladonna declared, her words resonating with a sense of limitless possibility. "Now, I would like to give you a demonstration.

Please direct your attention to the monitor behind me."

All eyes turned to the screen that displayed "Quantum Innovations, Where the Future Moves Beyond the Speed of Light."

ELEVEN

Ladonna Stone stood before the exhilarated audience, their applause echoing through the grand hall. The room was buzzing with anticipation, for they had just witnessed a glimpse of the future. A future that Ladonna had worked tirelessly to bring to fruition. But behind her poised demeanor and visionary leadership, there was a story—a tale of how Ladonna came to occupy the coveted position of CEO at Quantum Innovations. Five years earlier, in the illustrious city of Washington D.C., Ladonna, along with her boss, General Chad "The Reaper" Mosier, and her husband, Michael, found themselves engaged in conversation with none other than the President of the United States. Ladonna exuded confidence, grace, and a regal aura that caught the attention of one man in particular—Mr Thomas Landon Cline, the CEO of Quantum Innovations.

General Chad "The Reaper" Mosier, renowned for his tactical brilliance and unwavering dedication to combat efficiency, had earned his moniker during his illustrious career as a pilot in the Air Force. With countless successful missions under his belt, Reaper demonstrated an exceptional ability to devise strategic plans and think on his feet during intense combat situations.

Driven by his passion for technology, Reaper recognized the value it could bring to the battlefield. However, experience has taught him the importance of always having a contingency plan in case technology failed or unforeseen circumstances arose. He believed in leveraging technological advancements to enhance combat capabilities, but never relied solely on them, understanding the necessity of adaptability and alternative approaches.

As a visionary leader, Reaper's expertise and innovative mindset propelled him to key positions within the military hierarchy, ultimately leading him to become Ladonna's formidable boss at the Department of Defense. His extensive experience and unique perspective on the intersection of technology and warfare made him an invaluable asset in driving forward advancements in Defense systems and strategies.

As the evening unfolded, the discussion delved into diverse topics, including leadership and the qualities that define a successful CEO. Ladonna listened intently as Mr Cline shared his insights and she could not help but feel a sense of admiration for his wisdom and experience. Intrigued, she decided to dig deeper into Mr Cline's understanding of leadership.

"You know, Mr Cline, I recently read your book, 'What Makes a Good CEO'. The foreword of the book struck a chord within me.."

Ladonna paused for a moment, her eyes reflecting the depth of her connection to the words. "It was written by Pride Stephenson, a renowned futurist and visionary thinker. His words resonated with me because he captured the essence of embracing technology as a driving force for progress and transformation. He spoke of a future where innovation and leadership intersect to shape a better world." I remember the foreword.

Ladonna gathered her thoughts, and then continued, reciting the words from memory. "Dear reader, as we move into the future, technology will continue to play an increasingly vital role in our lives. The CEO of this company has been at the forefront of this technological revolution. He has a great understanding of leadership and what it takes to keep people driving forward. I am honored to have been asked to write the foreword for this book. In these pages, you will find insights into the future of technology and how it will shape our world. You will learn about the latest trends and innovations in the tech industry, and how they are changing the way we live and work. I hope that this book will inspire you to think differently about the future and embrace the opportunities that lie ahead.

Sincerely,

Pride Stephenson".

"I remember the entire book. But since you are the author, Ladonna said with a smile, "I suppose there is no need for me to recite it to you," Ladonna continued, Pride Stephenson believes that technology is not just a tool, but a catalyst for change. His foreword emphasized the importance of forward-thinking leaders who can harness the potential of technology to create a brighter future. It was an affirmation of my own beliefs and aspirations."

Mr Cline and the attentive bystanders found themselves captivated by her extraordinary recall and profound understanding of his book.

"Indeed, Pride Stephenson is a remarkable individual," Mr. Cline chimed in, his voice filled with admiration. "He possesses an unparalleled ability to envision the possibilities that lie ahead and inspire others to embrace those possibilities. I had the privilege of collaborating with him on several projects, and his insights have shaped my own perspective on leadership."

The conversation between Ladonna, Mr Cline, and Michael continued, weaving together anecdotes, ideas, and shared visions of the future. In that moment, a bond began to form—a connection built on mutual respect, intellectual curiosity, and a shared passion for driving innovation.

As they delved deeper into the intricacies of leadership and the potential for growth within Quantum Innovations, Mr Cline could not help but be captivated by Ladonna's astute observations and unique perspective. Her ability to see beyond the surface, to envision a world of limitless possibilities, was a quality he believed would be invaluable in the realm of leadership.

Ladonna did not know that her words and presence had been sealed in Mr Cline's mind. It was in that first meeting, within the hallowed halls of power, that he decided he wanted to pass the torch of leadership to Ladonna when the time was right. His belief in Ladonna's exceptional qualities was fortified, solidifying his conviction that she was the visionary leader Quantum Innovations needed to spearhead them into a new era of technological advancements.

Little did they know that their initial encounter would set in motion a series of events that would lead to Ladonna's ascendency to the CEO position and the battle for dominance that awaited her in the present.

Two years later, Ladonna had left her position at the Department of Defence and had formed a close friendship with Mr Cline. As they spent time together, Ladonna shared her passion for superposition, Quantum Entanglement, and other revolutionary concepts that could propel technology to unimaginable heights. Mr Cline, while in awe of the concept, admitted that it was beyond his understanding.

When Ladonna mentioned her plans to seek funding for her groundbreaking project, Mr Cline made a bold offer. He told her Quantum Innovations would fully fund her endeavour. Though hesitant at first, Ladonna ultimately accepted the proposition and thus began the arduous journey to turn her vision into reality.

Days turned into months as Ladonna oversaw the construction of the cutting-edge laboratory at her home. Immersed in her work, she faced countless setbacks and challenges, especially in the realm of temperature control for delicate qubits. Nevertheless, her sheer determination led her to explore unconventional approaches, ultimately resulting in a breakthrough. She succeeded in developing qubits that could withstand any temperature, a pivotal achievement that solidified her position as a trailblazer in the field.

When Ladonna shared her new direction with Mr Cline, he was at a crossroads in his own life. Contemplating retirement to spend more time with his family, he recognized the immense potential within Ladonna and her knowledge of Quantum Computing. In a heartfelt offer, he extended the position of CEO to Ladonna, who initially declined. However, Mr Cline persisted, sweetening the proposition by granting Ladonna the freedom to utilize the equipment of the Quantum Computing lab given her lab was limited by space and she was aware of the cutting-edge equipment at Quantum Innovations lab.

Ladonna finally accepted and the board eagerly supported the decision, having never met her but was infected with Mr Cline's praises of her and what she could ultimately bring to the company. They recognized the invaluable asset they would gain and unanimously voted to allow her to be CEO.

And so, within a matter of weeks, Ladonna assumed the role of CEO at Quantum Innovations. The stage was set for her to realize her vision and lead the company into a new era of innovation. The years of hard work, friendship, and extraordinary abilities had culminated in this moment. Her mind returned to the present. She reflected on the incredible journey that had brought her to this point. The applause in the room served as a testament to the impact she had already made.

TWELVE

After Ladonna made her presentation, raucous applause from the board members, Executives, and their esteemed guests greeted her. Her presentation had ignited their imaginations, opening their minds to the boundless possibilities that lie before them. The vision of a world where communication knew no boundaries and where technology seamlessly connected individuals and communities was becoming a reality. As the applause grew softer, Ladonna said, "Now, ladies and gentlemen, I would like to give you a demonstration of the power that lies within the Quantum OmniLink. Please direct your attention to the monitor behind me."

The screen displayed the words "Quantum Innovations: Where the Future Moves Beyond the Speed of Light". A captivating video began playing, depicting the Earth turning in the vastness of space. Clouds drifted across the screen, and a voice filled the room, carrying the promise of a new era of communication. It said, "What if you could speak to anyone, anywhere with your current mobile phone? No more reliance on satellite phones. No more disconnection from the world because you find yourself atop a mountain or deep within a forest."

The video zoomed in on a campsite nestled near the peak of Mount Everest. A group of mountaineers clad in their gears, the onlookers in the auditorium stood in awe of the majestic crystal-clear surroundings. One of the men in the video then took out his cell phone and dialed a number. Ladonna's phone rang, and it was none other than her husband, Michael, calling from the top of the world.

The voice of Michael echoed around the mountains clearly and devoid of any interruption or distortions. "Hello, dear, I just wanted to check up on you. We are here near the top of Mount Everest. How is the reception?" Ladonna's face lit up with joy upon hearing her husband's voice. "I can hear you loud and clear and so can everyone else. So, better have decorum, young man," she playfully responded. As their conversation proceeded, Michael's voice was soft and slow, "Take care of yourself up there, Ladonna. Remember, safety first." Ladonna smiled, her love for Michael was evident through the phone conversation. She said, "I will, Michael. Do not worry, I have got the best team with me. We will be fine."

With a graceful pause, Ladonna seamlessly transitioned from English to Thai, effortlessly expressing herself. She said,

"ขอบคุณนะครับไมเคิลทีโทรมาหาผมครับ ผมขอบคุณมากครับ" ("Thank you, Michael, for calling me. I appreciate it.") Her words flowed effortlessly in her second language, showcasing her linguistic versatility and the depth of her gratitude.

Then she asked Michael, "What language did you just hear?" He laughed and replied, "I heard you in English. Are you showing off all of the languages you speak?" She joined in his laughter and replied in French, "Tu me connaissi bien, mon merveilleux mari." (You know me so well, my wonderful husband.)

Ladonna's voice took on a tender tone as she addressed Michael directly, this time in Japanese, "マイケル、安全で素晴らしい冒険を楽しんでね！" (Michael, please be safe and have a great adventure!) Her message conveyed not only a plea for his safety but also the depth of her love, spoken in a language that resonated with their shared experiences. Michael, responded in English with a voice that carried affection. "It is my absolute pleasure. I will see you in a week. Kisses."

Ladonna chuckled, reverting to English. "Thank you, Michael. I appreciate you doing this. See you soon!"

After she disconnected the call, she could not resist sharing one more revelation, a testament to the limitless potential of the Quantum OmniLink system. She said, "Wait, there is one more remarkable feature of every Quantum OmniLink connection. Now, you might be wondering how we effortlessly switch between languages like Thai, French, and Japanese? Well, the truth is, while my husband does not speak Thai, French, or Japanese fluently, the Quantum OmniLink breaks down language barriers. It automatically translates our conversation in real-time to the language set in the device, allowing for seamless communication across different languages. With Quantum OmniLink, language barriers are a thing of the past. Moreover, the drone that captured this 12k footage seamlessly streamed its video feed through OmniLink, with such negligible latency that it seems to rivals the experience of witnessing it in person. But today, we have more to unveil. Our expedition into uncharted territories extends beyond the realm of communication. Quantum Innovations stands on the brink of revolutionizing other facets of our existence." The board members saw the technological revolution of the Quantum OmniLink System. The promise of seamless communication transcending languages and distances made them more intrigued about the ocean of wealth the Company is about to swim in. As the excitement continued with what lies ahead for the Company, Ladonna stepped aside from the centre stage, signaling Justin Allen to join her. The lights dimmed, engulfing the room in darkness, and all eyes turned to the monitor, which illuminated the stage with a vivid display.

A DNA strand appeared on the screen. Its intricate structure is coming into focus. The audience leaned forward, captivated by the profound implications of what they were about to witness, a voice emanated from the speakers, cool and confident as if from the future itself.

"The DNA strand has been computed," the voice declared. "There are genes in this sample that contain segments that are out of order. Given time this can lead to the development of ovarian cancer. Should I repair it?".

The question hung in the air, the weight of its implications sinking in. Justin, standing beside Ladonna, spoke with unwavering conviction. "Yes, repair it," he affirmed, his voice filled with determination. And then, the screen burst into a symphony of motion. In the bio sample before them there is a flurry of activities, like celestial dancers, unfolded before the mesmerized eyes of the board members. Millions of microscopic nanobots swarmed the DNA strand, their intricate movements synchronized in a mesmerizing display of precision. Each nanobot, not much larger than an adam, tirelessly worked its way along the strand, making microscopic changes with astonishing accuracy. Like master craftsmen, they delicately repaired the gene's anomaly, ensuring that every segment fell into perfect alignment. It was a symphony of synchronized movements, a ballet of technological marvels. As the nanobots performed their intricate dance, the room was bathed in a dazzling display of colors. Brilliant hues of blue, green, and gold illuminated the faces of the awe-struck audience, casting an ethereal glow that seemed to transcend the boundaries of the screen. Second by second, the profound transformation unfolded before their eyes, a mesmerizing display of technology and innovation. The scene playing out on the screen was not a pre-rendered video, but rather a real-time creation brought to life by a generative AI. As the nanobots, guided by the advanced Quantum algorithms, received trillions of commands sent through the Quantum OmniLink system, they embarked on their intricate mission to rectify the gene's flaw. With unrivaled precision and seamless coordination, the nanobots navigated the complex twists and turns of the DNA strand. Their actions were orchestrated by the Quantum computer, utilizing its immense processing power to analyze and determine the precise adjustments required for each segment. As the nanobots worked diligently, the commands flowing through the Quantum OmniLink system in real-time, their impact became evident. Delicate adjustments were made, minute alterations that gradually restored the DNA strand to its optimal state. It was a delicate dance, a symphony of microscopic changes orchestrated by the synergy of Quantum technology. The sheer complexity of the task was astonishing, yet the Quantum algorithms effortlessly managed every intricate detail. The nanobots seamlessly executed their mission, tirelessly repairing the gene's flaw with unwavering accuracy.

The room was enraptured, the audience leaning forward in anticipation as they witnessed the miraculous reconstruction unfolding before them. The power of the Quantum computer, and the OmniLink system, coupled with the ingenuity of the Quantum algorithms, and Quantum AI was revolutionizing the very essence of life itself. Second, by second, the DNA strand regained its integrity, each adjustment bringing it closer to its optimal state. It was a testament to the limitless potential of Quantum technology, a glimpse into a future where precision medicine and targeted therapies held the promise of unprecedented breakthroughs. As the transformation neared completion, the audience held their breath, their anticipation reaching a crescendo. And then, with the final adjustment made, the corrected gene shone brightly on the screen, a symbol of triumph and hope. The room erupted in thunderous applause, an outpouring of appreciation for the extraordinary achievement they had just witnessed. The board members, their faces radiant with wonder, exchanged glances of amazement, and their faith in the Quantum revolution solidified. In that transformative moment, the power of Quantum technology and the Quantum OmniLink system had not only repaired all the genes in the sample but had unveiled a world of possibilities. It was a testament to the profound impact they could have on human health, paving the way for personalized medicine, groundbreaking discoveries, and a future where the boundaries of scientific advancement knew no limits. The precision of their movements was awe-inspiring. They navigated the twists and turns of the DNA strand with unwavering accuracy, their actions guided by the power of Quantum Artificial Intelligence. It was a mesmerizing sight, a testament to the remarkable capabilities of technology harnessed for the betterment of humanity. And as quickly as they had arrived, the nanobots completed their task. Their work done, they dissolved into the bloodstream, their microscopic presence fading away without a trace. The repaired DNA strand stood as a testament to their incredible feat, an intricate tapestry of life's potential restored to its fullest. The room erupted in thunderous applause, a crescendo of awe and admiration for the marvel they had witnessed. The board members, their eyes filled with wonder, exchanged glances of amazement and excitement. It was a moment that would forever be etched in their memories, a turning point in the history of scientific achievement. Ladonna, standing at the forefront of this groundbreaking moment, felt a surge of pride and gratitude. She had envisioned a world where technology could heal, where the boundaries of human potential could be pushed to new frontiers. And now, before her, that vision had become a reality.

"Now, my esteemed board members," Ladonna began, her voice filled with wonder and excitement, "what you have witnessed is just the beginning. With brilliant members like Justin, the power of the Quantum computer, the Quantum OmniLink system, and the remarkable capabilities of Quantum Artificial Intelligence, we call it the Quantum trinity, we have the potential to revolutionize not only the field of medicine but countless other areas of human endeavor." The applause continued, echoing throughout the room, as the magnitude of their achievement settled in. Ladonna knew that the journey ahead would be filled with challenges and unexplored territories, but with each step they took, the world grew more wondrous and full of possibilities. Together, they had glimpsed the true power of the Quantum Revolution. It was a revolution not only in technology but in the way they perceived the limits of human potential. And with every barrier they shattered, they brought humanity closer to a future where miracles were not just the stuff of dreams but the reality they had the power to create.

As the screen displayed the corrected gene, the room fell into a hushed silence, the air thick with anticipation. Then, with a surge of radiant light, the voice resumed its words a symphony of wonder and possibility.

"What if…"

The voice echoed through the room, its cadence carrying the weight of untold potential. The words ignited the imaginations of the board members, their minds soaring to new heights, envisioning a world where dreams once deemed unthinkable became tangible realities. The screen became a canvas, alive with a mesmerizing dance of images, each one a gateway to extraordinary possibilities. Text flashed across the screen, a mesmerizing tapestry that wove together the threads of innovation and boundless imagination.

"What if you could have surgery where you only had to take a pill?" The words reverberated, sending ripples of wonder through the room. The screen unveiled a vision of the future where precision machines, minuscule in size, held the power to revolutionize medical procedures. With dimensions as small as one or two molecules in diameter, these remarkable creations, guided by the brilliance of Quantum Artificial Intelligence, would venture into the depths of the human body, targeting and repairing damaged tissue from within. The audience found themselves transported to a realm where traditional surgical interventions gave way to a new era of non-invasive treatments, where the mere act of swallowing a pill held the potential to transform lives. The room buzzed with excitement, minds ablaze with the boundless possibilities that lay ahead.

What if the development of drugs could be accelerated to unimaginable speeds, enabling targeted therapies and personalized medications? The screen morphed into a panorama of medical breakthroughs, revealing Quantum Computers as the catalysts of a paradigm shift in drug discovery. Through their ability to simulate the behavior of molecules, these extraordinary machines would fast-track research, leading to faster and more precise drug development for ailments that plagued humanity, such as Cancer, Parkinson, and Alzheimer's. The room was awash with awe, the vision of a future where diseases that once eluded our grasp were finally conquered.

What if we could predict the weather so accurately that we would know precisely where to put wind farms, where to plant crops, and exactly what crops would grow best and in what location? A breathtaking landscape unfolded, vibrant with wind farms positioned precisely where the elements converged, harnessing the earth's energy in perfect harmony. Fields of crops flourished, nourished by the knowledge of what to plant, where to plant, and when to plant. The vision of an interconnected ecosystem, where Quantum technology provided the tools to predict and shape nature itself, stirred the hearts of the audience. They could almost taste the fruits of a world where human ingenuity and the power of the Quantum computer harmonized with the rhythm of the natural world.

What if the sensitivity and precision of sensors could be pushed to new frontiers? The screen transformed once again, revealing a tapestry of advancements in various fields. Medical imaging, once limited in its scope, now offered unprecedented clarity, allowing doctors to peer into the depths of the human body with unparalleled precision. Environmental monitoring systems became beacons of hope, safeguarding the delicate balance of our planet by detecting even the slightest changes in our surroundings. Navigation systems guided explorers and travelers with unwavering accuracy, eliminating uncertainty and charting paths of discovery. The audience was spellbound, their minds grappling with the infinite possibilities that these advancements presented.

All these what-ifs are no longer distant fantasies but tangible visions within reach. The remarkable power of Quantum Computers, the Quantum OmniLink system, and Artificial Intelligence, The Quantum Trinity, fortified by the genius of the minds at Quantum Innovations, promised a future where limitations were shattered, and human potential soared to unprecedented heights. In that transcendent moment, the board members found themselves standing on the precipice of a new epoch, a journey into uncharted territories of human progress. Their hearts swelled with wonder, dreams taking flight on the wings of innovation. The voice's words lingered in the air, carrying the collective aspirations of a world on the cusp of transformation. And as the applause filled the room once again, it was not merely a tribute to the accomplishments of the present but a resounding ovation to the limitless potential of the future.

The room fell into a hushed silence, the words hanging in the air like a melody that lingered. The board members sat transfixed, their minds spinning with the possibilities that had been unveiled. The boundaries of science and human potential had been shattered, revealing a world of untold wonders. Ladonna, standing at the forefront of this extraordinary revolution, felt a surge of pride and exhilaration. The room erupted with applause, the sound thunderous and filled with awe. The Quantum Revolution had begun, and the journey ahead promised to be as breathtaking as the moment they had just experienced. "Now, my esteemed board members," Ladonna declared, her voice resolute and filled with wonder, "you have witnessed the birth of a new era. The Quantum Trinity has come together to reshape our world. The future has arrived, and it is more extraordinary than we could have ever imagined."

The applause continued, the excitement unmistakable. Ladonna knew that the path ahead would be filled with challenges and triumphs, but she was ready to lead Quantum Innovations into this brave new world. With the Quantum Revolution at their side, they were poised to unlock the full potential of human ingenuity and reshape the course of history.

The future had arrived, and Ladonna is its vanguard, ready to reshape the fabric of society and push the boundaries of human achievement. The world would never be the same again.

The applause still echoed through the grand hall as Ladonna smiled graciously, reveling in her presentation's triumphant reception. But her attention was abruptly drawn to the rear of the room. The double doors had swung open, revealing an imposing figure adorned in the regalia of a five-star

General. Murmurs rippled through the crowd at the unknown man's sudden arrival. He was flanked on either side by armed soldiers, their presence amplifying the tension. Ladonna observed with interest - his weathered face and piercing gaze seemed distantly familiar.

Jackson Reed, Ladonna's chief of security, adeptly moved to intercept the unexpected guests. "General, welcome. This is certainly a surprise. How may I assist you?" he inquired, unphased by the contingent's foreboding appearance.

The general's gravelly voice cut sharply through the uneasy atmosphere. "I must speak with Ladonna Stone immediately regarding a matter of urgent national security." His steely eyes scanned the room until they locked onto Ladonna's.

Comprehension dawned on her, paired with a sense of unease. This was no stranger - it was General Chad "The Reaper" Mosier, her former mentor and commanding officer from her shadowy days working in clandestine government projects before Quantum Innovations. His unannounced presence could only mean something was terribly wrong.

Ladonna exchanged a subtle nod with Jackson, signaling her intent to comply with the request. She stepped forward, maintaining an aura of confidence. "General Mosier, what an unexpected honor. Let us speak somewhere more private." His stern expression told her this was no courtesy call. From resent conversations she had some idea what it was about.

As they briskly exited the hall, Mosier leaned in and murmured cryptically, "You possess knowledge critical in averting a catastrophic threat. I'll explain the details shortly." His words sent a chill down her spine.

And with that, the stage was set for a new chapter, a twist in the tale, as Ladonna ventured into uncharted territory. Her destiny intertwined with the secrets and revelations that awaited her in the presence of the mysterious General.

The closing of this chapter marked not an end but a beginning. It was a prelude to a future fraught with uncertainty, danger, and untold possibilities. The legacy of Ladonna Stone and Quantum Innovations would now be tested like never before.